A DEADLY EXCHANGE

"Hold still!" a voice snapped.

Joe's blood froze in his veins. That was the voice of the Haiduk!

Bess screamed again in the darkness, this time in pain.

"I said, hold *still!*" the harsh, grating voice ordered.

The scuffling stopped, but Joe could hear little whimpers coming from the captured girl.

"All right." The Haiduk's voice sounded confident in the pitch blackness. "I have Ms. Marvin held quite securely . . . and my weapon is pointed at her head. I understand you're quite fond of this young woman, Prince Casimir. Well, we'll see how far you're willing to go for her."

The voice in the darkness grew cold. Everyone was motionless and silent.

"Because, unless you show yourself in ten seconds, Ms. Marvin dies!"

Nancy Drew & Hardy Boys SuperMysteries

Available from ARCHWAY Paperbacks

A NANCY AND HARDY DREW BOYS SUPER MYSTERY™

ROYAL REVENGE

Carolyn Keene

AN ARCHWAY PAPERBACK
Published by POCKET BOOKS
New York London Toronto Sydney Tokyo Singapore

AN ARCHWAY PAPERBACK *Original*

 An Archway Paperback published by
POCKET BOOKS, a division of Simon & Schuster Inc.
1230 Avenue of the Americas, New York, NY 10020

Copyright © 1997 by Simon & Schuster Inc.
Produced by Mega-Books, Inc.

ISBN: 0-671-00735-1

First Archway Paperback printing December 1997

10 9 8 7 6 5 4 3 2 1

NANCY DREW, THE HARDY BOYS, AN ARCHWAY PAPERBACK and colophon are registered trademarks of Simon & Schuster Inc.

A NANCY DREW AND HARDY BOYS SUPERMYSTERY is a trademark of Simon & Schuster Inc.

Cover art by Franco Accornero

Printed in the U.S.A.

IL 6+

Chapter

One

"IT'S WEIRD," George Fayne said to her friends Bess Marvin and Nancy Drew as they moved quickly along the broken pavement in the crisp fall night air. "I've lived in River Heights all my life, and I've never been in this neighborhood before."

"According to Hannah, we've all been missing out by not coming here," Nancy reported. Hannah Gruen, the Drews' housekeeper, had just about raised Nancy after Nancy's mother passed away fifteen years earlier. "There's a bakery here that makes the best pastries in River Heights. Hannah used to take me to it when I was young, and I still remember how excited I'd get. It was a big adventure for a little kid."

"It's still quite an adventure," Bess piped up.

1

"At least, it has been for me. Hannah's right. We were missing out, and that's why I wanted to bring you guys here."

George stole a glance in the soft evening darkness at her cousin. It was unlike Bess to be so enthusiastic about anyplace, especially one as run-down as Little Panaslava appeared to be. "Hannah said it was like another country here. Too bad it looks like such a poor one."

"George!" Bess scolded. "What a rotten thing to say."

"Come on, Bess," George said, defending herself. "There's broken glass and litter all over the sidewalks, not to mention boarded-up windows in abandoned buildings. Not even the dark can blur the signs of neglect."

"You have to learn to look beyond the surface, George Fayne," her cousin answered.

Nancy could tell she and George were thinking the same thought: Was this the Bess they'd known all their lives? They both shook their heads.

Bess continued. "Little Panaslava has always been an immigrant neighborhood, mostly Eastern European. The people came to River Heights for jobs in factories that are now closed. Ever since the Panaslavan Communist government fell, there's been a new wave of immigrants to River Heights. We don't have jobs for them anymore. So you can't expect Little Panaslava to look prosperous."

Bess's speech stopped Nancy and George in

their tracks. Bess couldn't remember when the Declaration of Independence was signed. How could she know about immigration trends of the late twentieth century in River Heights?

"How did you learn all this, Bess?" Nancy asked.

"Yeah," George chimed in. "I didn't know that *history* was a word in your vocabulary."

Nancy could tell from Bess's grin that she'd been waiting to impress her friends.

" 'Fess up, Bess," Nancy said. "Have you been watching PBS again?"

"No," Bess said. "I've brought you to Little Panaslava to hear a great band and"—she paused—"to meet someone."

"Bess, now you've got me scared," George said. "First history and now ethnic music?"

Nancy hissed at George. "You weren't listening. She said, 'a great band *and* to meet someone,' as in a *guy.*"

"Oh, I get it!" George slapped her forehead. "It all makes sense now. Sudden interest in Panaslavan history plus Panaslavan music equals . . ."

Nancy joined George in finishing her sentence. "A Panaslavan guy!"

"Hey," Bess complained, "that's not fair, but, okay, it's true. Come on, let's go—and not another bad word out of either of you."

As they walked under a streetlight, the girls passed a storefront window with the word *Mesar* painted on it in old-fashioned gold lettering.

Under that was taped up a piece of paper with the handwritten word *Meat*.

"I don't think they need the translation," George said. "Not with all those chunks of animal hanging in the window. Look at those poor naked things without their fur—I think they were rabbits."

Bess didn't pay any more attention to her cousin. She pointed across the street. "There it is."

The "it" was a club that was located in the cellar of an old brick building. The door, which was down a short flight of steps, looked like every other unmarked cellar door on the block.

After passing through the thick, fortresslike opening, Nancy paused in surprise. The inside of the club was nothing like its grim exterior. Special lighting illuminated tiny silver speckles that seemed to be everywhere—on the walls and ceiling, on the leather-and-chrome chairs, and even on the floor.

The walls of the club were painted an almost black purple near the entrance. The color gradually lightened until, at the far end of the room, the walls had become blazing red. Against this bright color stood a stage, and between the stage and the front door, the room was filled with a crowd in their late teens and early twenties.

"Check it out!" George muttered.

"You're not going to hear balalaikas here," Bess said smugly.

As the girls made their way to a table near the

front, lights came up on the stage. A young man in a battered leather jacket and ripped jeans walked casually up to the microphone at center stage and tossed back his long blond hair.

"Hey," he called to the audience. "I think we're ready. How about you?" The crowd burst into cheers, whistles, and applause. "All right!" cried the emcee. "And now, who did we all come to hear?"

Obviously, the local crowd knew the routine. Bess joined them in a huge communal response: "Incognito!"

Before the shout had died down, four young men stepped onto the stage. As they settled in, a chant arose: "Incogni-*to!* Incogni-*to!*"

Nancy was surprised at how normal the band looked. She had expected something a little different from the faded, worn jeans, plaid flannel shirts, and long hair—

"A grunge band?" George blurted out.

The guy on lead guitar nodded to the other band members, then stomped a rhythm on the stage with a heavy motorcycle boot. It was joined by a blistering bass beat, and soon Incognito rocked into its version of an old Led Zeppelin tune.

Nancy moved to the music. "Not bad!" she yelled over the amplified sound.

The lead guitarist was also the singer. He had a powerful, slightly raw-sounding voice. Nancy couldn't identify his accent, but it was definitely not Slavic. Perhaps British, she thought.

What's he doing here, especially in Little Panaslava? Nancy wondered. She turned to ask Bess, but her friend's attention was glued to the stage, or, more precisely, to the lead singer.

Ah-ha, Nancy thought. That's the Panaslavan guy, but why no accent?

Well, the guy was good-looking. His moves showed off his great muscle tone, and his intense, chiseled features were set off by long jet-black hair. He seemed to Nancy to be a handsome, classic Greek statue come to life.

Nancy glanced over at Bess again and could almost feel the intensity radiating from her. Yep, Nancy thought, Bess has really fallen for this guy.

The band continued with a couple of other well-known tunes—a Metallica song and a real head-banging number by Megadeth.

Then people in the crowd began calling out requests for songs Nancy had never heard of. "'Ocean Between Us'!" a guy yelled.

Bess shouted, "'She's a Lady'!"

The lead singer smiled at her and nodded. "'She's a Lady,'" he agreed.

The song was a bluesy love song, and Bess's smile couldn't have been bigger.

"These guys aren't your average garage band," George pronounced as the song ended. "That guitarist is hot."

Bess nodded proudly. "They've sent audition tapes to a couple of major record companies," she said. "Cass thinks Incognito is on the verge of a contract."

"Cass?" George inquired.

"The lead guitarist," Bess said. "You'll meet him in a minute."

George looked at Nancy for confirmation. "Did I miss something?" she asked.

Nancy nodded affirmatively. "Guitarist equals Panaslavan guy" was all she said.

As soon as Incognito finished its first set and left the stage, Bess had Nancy and George on their feet and heading toward the dressing rooms.

Backstage reminded Nancy of a gym locker room—especially when they found Bess's handsome guitarist rubbing his bare torso down with a towel.

Bess went right up to him and kissed his cheek. "Nancy Drew, George Fayne, meet Cass Carroll."

Cass nodded politely but didn't act thrilled at seeing either Bess or her friends invade his private space. Maybe Bess was pushing too hard with this guy, Nancy thought.

"Would you like to go to that little coffee shop down the block, Cass?" Bess suggested softly. "It would give you guys a chance to get to know one another."

Now Cass Carroll seemed even less comfortable. "Okay. I need to clean up a bit, though." He softened a little and gave the girls a truly killer smile. "I'm afraid rocking is sweaty work."

Nancy and Bess waited by the entrance to the club while George paid their bill. "Bess," Nancy said carefully, "was it a good idea to spring us on Cass like that?"

Bess had stars in her eyes. "Cass and I have been going out for a couple of weeks now, and I just couldn't keep it a secret anymore."

Nancy didn't like the idea of secrets, either. "So what's the story with Cass?"

Bess grinned, eyes sparkling. "He's a man of mystery. Just try asking him some questions."

"That doesn't sound good, Bess." Nancy frowned. "Men of mystery sometimes have mysterious extra girlfriends."

"No way!" Bess shook her head. "I've seen enough of Cass and the guys in the band to be sure of that. Oh! Here they come."

George joined them, and so did Cass, now in a fresh flannel shirt and a hooded red sweatshirt. "I can only spend a little time with you," he apologized. "We've got to go back on in half an hour. And there's supposed to be a guy from one of the record companies here tonight."

They walked down a block lined with old stores that had been converted into homes. Nancy could see bits of flaking gold paint on the old windowsills, which framed sagging blinds, and, here and there, blankets used as drapes.

At the end of the block was a big plate-glass window from which warm light streamed. Nancy had been expecting some sort of diner, but instead she entered a turn-of-the-century coffee bar with blindingly clean white walls and dark wood tables and chairs. Glittering coffee machines, reflected in a large mirror, were each brewing a different blend. The mingled aromas of coffee and pastries were heavenly.

They were greeted at the door by an elegant older man with a hawklike nose and thinning silver hair brushed straight back. In spite of his age, he stood tall and straight.

"Welcome to Egon's," he said in a slight Pana-slavan accent as he bowed to the girls. Then he shook a finger at Cass. *"Three* young ladies now? Please sit down here." He led them to one of the larger tables. "No need to order. Egon brings the best in the house!"

Moments later they were sipping strong, sweet coffee from fine china cups with gold rims. The golden pastries that accompanied the coffee were equally delicious. Nancy's first bite filled her mouth with light, buttery pastry dough and drenched her taste buds in warm apricot filling.

"Delicious!" Nancy declared. "Cass, how did you find this place?"

"It's the other way around," Cass said with a grin. "Old Egon found me. He's kind to starving artists." He winked. "Besides, the pastry would go stale if someone didn't eat it."

"How did you and Bess meet?" George asked abruptly. Nancy frowned at her lack of tact, and George responded with an innocent look that Nancy read as I-just-want-to-know-don't-you?

"It was at the Seven-Eleven," Bess said.

"I work there," Cass explained. "My day job, you see."

As he laughed, Nancy again wondered about what she had definitely identified as Cass's British accent. Bess might joke, but this guy *was* a man of mystery—a Panaslavan with an American job and an English accent, hanging out in an Eastern European neighborhood.

Nancy was trying to figure out how to ask for some answers, when Egon came rushing out of the kitchen. His smile had disappeared, and his face was gray. "On the overseas radio—I hear—" He had suddenly lost his almost perfect English. "King Boris—shot dead in Paris!"

An elderly woman at one of the other tables burst into tears. But most of the people in the café—especially the younger ones—said, "King who?"

"I don't understand," Nancy said. "I thought that Panaslava had been broken up into six separate republics since the Communists—"

Cass interrupted. "Before the Communists, a king ruled Panaslava. Boris was this king's son—the pretender to the throne." His upper lip twisted as if he'd tasted something bad. "I guess that's over now, if he's dead."

The young man rose so quickly, he almost knocked the table over. Before anyone could follow, he was out of the café.

Chapter

Two

A DAY EARLIER and a thousand miles away, Frank and Joe Hardy sat watching a videotape in their Bayport living room. The film playing was a science-fiction epic they both had seen a dozen times. Trumpets blazed as the grim-faced hero, dressed all in black, raised his laser sword and charged to the rescue of the Galactic Princess.

"What is it that makes girls get so goofy about princes and princesses?" The question escaped from Joe Hardy, who lay sprawled on the couch. A scowl darkened his handsome, slightly square blond features.

"Do I have to answer that right now, during one of the best parts of the movie?" Joe's older brother, Frank, asked. His leaner features hid a grin as his brown eyes took in Joe's annoyance.

Sighing, Frank hit the pause button. "Satisfied? Now, what are you talking about?"

"My last date with Vanessa was sabotaged by a prince," Joe complained.

Frank laughed. "Now, *this* I've got to hear. How did you and Vanessa meet a prince?"

"On the VCR," Joe growled. "I stopped by to pick her up. Her mom was putting on a tape she'd rented—*The Prisoner of Zenda* or something. The thing was in black and white and had to be at least sixty years old. There were all these guys in fancy military uniforms and thin mustaches, girls in long gowns—and, of course, a prince."

His scowl got deeper. "Vanessa started watching as she put on her coat. Then, all at once, she sat down. Then the coat came off, and we ended up missing the movie we were going to see. Vanessa and her mother were both crying over this prince at the end. So, I repeat, what is it with girls?"

"Couldn't tell you," Frank said, starting the video again. "Here comes the princess now—in her brass bikini."

Joe groaned, and Frank stopped the movie again. "Maybe it's because we *don't* have royalty that Americans go loony for princes and princesses. Look at the coverage the papers and gossip shows give to the British royal family."

Fenton Hardy, the boys' father, stuck his head into the room. "Excuse me for butting in, but I could hear you from the kitchen. People like to look back with fondness on times that they feel were more glamorous than the present."

He smiled. "Back when *The Prisoner of Zenda* was first written, most of the countries in Europe were still monarchies. In fact, there was a real boom in the king business back then."

"What do you mean, Dad?" Joe asked.

"Between 1840 and 1900, nearly a dozen new countries were created as the Ottoman Empire lost its hold on southeastern Europe, or the Balkan peninsula. Greece, Romania, Bulgaria, Rurithenia—all those countries were given kings from various existing royal families."

"Didn't the people who lived in those countries have any choice?" Frank asked.

"Not really," Fenton Hardy responded. "In those days, royalty pretty much called the shots. If there was a vacant throne, someone would put in a royal relative." He thought for a second. "Except Sarabia, the country that later became part of Panaslava. They had a home-grown leader who proclaimed himself king. And there was also another little country down there that was ruled by a prince who promoted himself to king."

"So what happened to all these royal families?" Joe wanted to know.

"World War One must have put a lot of them out of business, right, Dad?" Frank said.

Fenton Hardy nodded and picked up the rest of the story. "World War Two finished the job on the Balkan kingdoms. Almost all those countries were taken over by Communist regimes, and then the royal families were forced into exile."

"Bummer!" Joe said. "What do you do after you used to run a whole country?"

"Try to get it back?" Frank suggested with a grin.

"Maybe—but how long can you keep that up?" Joe said.

"You'd be surprised," Fenton Hardy suggested. "The czar of Russia was deposed in 1917. But a member of the Romanovs, the imperial family, was back in the country as soon as the Communists fell."

"But that stuff's, like, ancient history," Joe objected.

"I don't know," Frank said. "I read in the paper that some people are asking the guy who's supposed to be king of Panaslava to come in and help negotiate a peace there."

"It would be nice if he could help." Fenton Hardy shook his head. "With the Communists gone, things have gotten even nastier in some Balkan countries. I was just on the phone with a friend from Washington. He used to watch the embassy of the People's Republic of Rurithenia because they ran spy networks for the old Soviets. My friend says it's even worse now. The Rurithenian government is hiring out its old Cold War spies as hit men."

"You're kidding!" Joe blurted out.

His father looked grim. "I only wish I were.

14

The Rurithenians had a top-notch assassin, an agent code-named the Haiduk."

"Hosh—Hojj—how do you say that?" Joe asked.

"It comes out sort of like Hozh-duke," Fenton Hardy replied. "Haiduk is an old name for a combination bandit and freedom fighter who fought against the Turks in the Balkans. The Turks were always trying to make headway in the Balkans, and they were also a pretty bloodthirsty group." He looked unhappy. "In the days of communism, the Haiduk specialized in taking out Rurithenian exiles in supposedly safe countries—like here. Now, if he's working freelance . . ."

Shaking his head again, Fenton Hardy walked out of the living room. The boys went back to their video, but they'd lost their enthusiasm for it.

After supper that evening, the Hardys returned their video. They were heading down Oak Street toward home when Joe spotted a car turning onto the street behind them. He'd noticed a similar car outside the video store. It was a modest late-model sedan, with a whip antenna for a two-way radio and Washington, D.C., plates.

"Don't look now," he told Frank, who was behind the wheel. "But we've got a fed coming up on our back bumper."

"Maybe it's someone to see Dad," Frank suggested as he pulled into the driveway of the house. The government car turned in right behind them.

"Or maybe it's someone from the Network," Joe added, quickly slipping out of the van. He and Frank had helped the Network, a top-secret government intelligence agency, on a number of cases. But he didn't recognize the lone man emerging from the sedan.

Usually, their contact was an almost aggressively ordinary-looking agent called the Gray Man. This guy was a stranger, though he wore a dark suit, the unofficial uniform of a government man. He topped Frank's six-foot-one by a couple of inches of hard, lean muscle.

The stranger's jowls softened the line of his jaw. Maybe he wasn't the Gray Man, but he certainly looked ordinary enough. His dark hair was receding, and his eyes were almost colorless.

The guy would have been a perfect spy, Joe thought. But then, he could be some sort of bureaucrat coming to see Fenton.

"Frank and Joe Hardy?" the man asked.

The Hardys nodded, and Joe's eyes narrowed. Whoever this guy was, he hadn't come calling on Fenton Hardy.

Pulling a scuffed wallet from his jacket, the man showed them a government ID card. He was from the State Department. "Chuck Bascomb, special investigator. I'm involved in a case where you may be able to help."

"We don't generally have much to do with the diplomatic corps," Frank said.

"This, unfortunately, is a case of diplomatic crime," Bascomb replied. "Panaslavan extremists are using an embassy security agent, codenamed the Haiduk—"

"The Panaslavans have a Haiduk, too?" Joe broke in. "I thought that was a Rurithenian code name."

Bascomb was surprised, then impressed. "The Haiduk *is* a Rurithenian agent," he admitted.

"So his government isn't just hiring out their agents as hit men—they're actually taking jobs for other countries, as well," Frank said.

Bascomb gave them a crooked smile. "It seems you're better informed than I expected."

"But all we know about this guy is his code name," Joe said. "So I don't know how we can help you."

"Unfortunately, our information is also incomplete," Bascomb said. "We don't know who the Haiduk's target is. But we do know where he's going. You boys have knowledge of and connections in the midwestern town to which the Haiduk has been sent."

Frank and Joe exchanged shocked glances. There was only one place in the Midwest where Joe and Frank had connections. "You mean River Heights, outside of Chicago?"

The government agent nodded. "Excellent. You can be of assistance when we get there."

Chapter

Three

Ach, what a fool I am, blurting out the news like that!"

Nancy turned as Egon was rushing by their table and heading for the door.

"So, what's the story with Guitar Boy?" George asked as Egon passed.

The café owner stopped, taken aback by George's apparent rudeness. "Young Cass is a musician—an artist," he said somewhat defensively. "Who knows what will upset an artist?"

The tall, slim man gave an elegant shrug and recovered his cool.

So why did Nancy have such a hard time believing Egon's explanation of Cass's strange behavior?

In spite of his smile, the older man seemed

nervous. He kept stealing glances through the café's window at any sign of movement.

"A terrible night for Panaslava—such a terrible thing, that someone should kill the king!" he murmured.

"I know people still call this neighborhood Little Panaslava," Nancy said. "But I'm surprised to hear anyone talk about it as a nation anymore. Hasn't Panaslava split into about six separate countries?"

"My father fought to create Panaslava," Egon replied, turning to Nancy. "It is the country where I was born." He gave another one of his expressive shrugs. "Others may call their remaining little bits the Sarabian Republic, Korassia, Pannonia, Cerce-Kamen, or whatever else. But surely I can speak of my homeland by the name *I* remember."

"Do you remember King Boris as well?" Nancy asked.

"Not young Boris—the one who was just killed—but his father," Egon replied. "Nowadays, those who remember call him the Old King." A sad little smile passed over his face. "Just as they call me Old Egon."

Nancy got the feeling he was changing the subject intentionally.

"If you don't mind, I think I'll call you Uncle Egon," Nancy said, matching his smile.

Egon laughed. "I would like that very much, but not Uncle. Call me *Dedya* Egon, Grandfather

Egon, and I will be a wise grandfather for you, Miss . . ."

"Drew," Nancy said, offering her hand. "Nancy Drew."

"Natalya." Egon repeated her name in his own dialect. "Mudrashka Natalya." He paused before translating. "Granddaughter Nancy."

The woman who had cried out at the news of King Boris's death laughed behind her handkerchief and said something quickly in the language she and Egon shared. From the sound of it, she was teasing Egon. He spoke back to her sternly, and she returned to her coffee without glancing up again.

Though Nancy knew the woman must have been teasing Egon about her, she felt that Dedya Egon and Mudrashka Natalya had formed a bond.

"This is my friend George," Nancy continued.

"It's short for Georgia," George explained with a sigh, taking in Egon's perplexed look.

"And I suppose you already know Bess," Nancy finished with a glance at her worried friend.

"Indeed, Miss Bess has been here a time or two," Egon said diplomatically.

"So, Dedya Egon, why do you think someone would want to kill King Boris?" Nancy asked.

The café owner slid his hand into the pocket of his double-breasted blazer; his thumb remained outside the pocket. "It seems strange indeed," Egon said. "Unless the rumors I have heard were true. Some of the factions back home were asking young Boris to lead peace talks."

"Asking help from a king who hasn't been allowed into the country for more than fifty years?" Nancy asked in surprise.

"The king is one of the few things these little states have in common—besides the Communists," Egon replied. "My country was built from several provinces torn from old empires and two small nations after the Great War—what you call World War One. My father believed in the Pan-Slavic ideal. He thought that all the Slavic peoples could live peacefully united. But the reality was much harder than he ever expected. Panaslava had two different alphabets, three different religions, four different languages, and at least five separate nationalities."

The old man's eyes seemed focused on something far away, and a sad smile played across his expressive lips. "You might say we were a civil war waiting to happen." He sighed. "Although our peoples were all of the same Slavic family, there was too much history between them.

"Memories are very long in Panaslava," Egon went on. "Blood feuds can go on for generations. Four and five hundred years ago, the Turks invaded Europe. They took Greece, Bulgaria, Romania, and parts of Italy, and attacked deep into Austria."

"And the countries that later made up Panaslava," Nancy added.

Egon nodded. "Korassia turned to the Austrians. In Cerce-Kamen, the people joined with the Turks, even adopting their Muslim religion. Sarabia—once a strong and powerful kingdom—its people could only bow their heads and wait for a better day."

The old man smiled. "And a few retreated to the green mountains, Zelenogora, in my language. They fought on and were never conquered." He brought a clenched hand to his chest in a fierce patriotic gesture. "That is where I was born—Zelenogora."

"This stuff happened hundreds of years ago," George marveled. "But you talk about it as if it were yesterday."

Egon gave her an ironic smile. "Well, perhaps not yesterday. But all my people have is their history and a long memory. They fight over who gave in and who kept resisting, over whose kingdom was stronger when." He shook his head. "And every generation since, each nationality has added new sins that others feel they must avenge."

"Even in Zelenogora?" Nancy asked.

"I was a child when we were invaded by the Nazis. My father was murdered—by Korassian collaborators—for resisting them. The Old King had me smuggled out of the country, but I saw terrible things." Old Egon's face was bleak. "And that was not the worst that happened."

Egon shook his head, as if to dismiss painful memories. "Now, things just as terrible are happening again. Wars are breaking out constantly among these newly formed governments, and civil wars within the various countries, too. If the king had been able to stop them by talking peace, well, it would have been a great accomplishment."

For a moment, there was silence around the table. Nancy saw Bess glance from her watch to the doorway.

I bet she's heard barely a word Egon's been saying, Nancy thought. All she's been doing is worrying about Cass.

As if on cue, Bess burst out, "Where is he?"

"Maybe he went back to the club," George suggested. "He has to play another set, doesn't he?"

"Cass wouldn't just dump us," Bess insisted. "Sometimes he takes off when he's upset, but he should have been back by now."

Nancy turned to the café owner. "I guess you must know Cass pretty well, Dedya Egon. He hangs out here. I hear you even feed him."

Egon laughed, but Nancy detected that sudden nervousness again. "You might say I adopted him. A nice young man, a stranger in town—"

"Someone who might not be in this country legally," Nancy suggested mildly.

Old Egon drew back with a frown. "That is not a polite thing to say in a neighborhood of immigrants, Natalya," he scolded. Then his ironic smile returned. "For some of the new immigrants, it may be true. But not for Cass."

"I've got to go and find him," Bess announced abruptly, rising from her seat.

"What do we owe you, Dedya Egon?" Nancy asked, with a concerned eye on her friend.

"For friends of young Cass . . ." Egon said, and then finished his sentence by waving away Nancy's money.

Nancy thanked him. Then she and George took off after Bess, who was already out the door.

The streetlights were old-fashioned and dim and the side streets thick with shadows.

Bess looked up and down the block. "Where is he?" she cried. "Where did he go?"

"George is probably right. Let's check the club," Nancy suggested. They quickly headed back down the block. Downstairs in the rock club, the members of Incognito had taken over the table where the girls had been sitting. They'd pulled over another table to accommodate their friends.

"Danilo!" Bess cried, rushing up to the drummer. "Where's Cass?"

Danilo's long dirty-blond hair was pulled back in a ponytail. He stared at the girls in mock confusion. "Did he come back, Gavi?"

The lanky bass player looked up from the girl he was flirting with and shrugged. "I didn't see him. Did you, Milek? Hey, Milek!"

Incognito's curly-haired keyboard man put on a pair of glasses and was hunched over a piece of paper, writing music. He jumped as if somebody had burst his thought balloon and gazed around in surprise. "Last I knew, he left with you girls. He hasn't come back for the next set."

Bess immediately headed for the door. "Something is wrong," she insisted. "We've got to find Cass."

"Bess, take it easy," Nancy advised, trying to slow down the rising panic in her frantic friend. "If you want to catch Cass, maybe we should just wait here. After all," she added, "he said there might be someone from a record company here at the club. Don't you think—"

Bess wouldn't be stopped. She grabbed Nancy's hand and dragged her out onto the street. The three friends walked for a block, Bess calling Cass's name.

"Cass, please. Where are you?" she cried, her voice betraying that she was on the verge of tears.

"Looking for someone?" a lazy voice asked.

A young man stepped out of a patch of shadow from an alleyway. He was tall and rangy and wore a shiny fake leather jacket and tight black jeans. As he swaggered up to the girls, Nancy noticed he had on the same kind of motorcycle boots that Cass wore.

The guy might have been handsome except for his blond hair, which had been badly cut to a short fuzz, and the fact that his face was slightly pinched-looking. The rest of his body made Nancy think his gaunt face wasn't from lack of food. And then there was the scar.

It wasn't all that big, maybe an inch long from

the right corner of his mouth down toward his jaw. However he'd gotten it, the scar had left his lip twisted, freezing the right side of his face in a slight smirk.

Definitely creepy, Nancy thought.

The smirk stretched to the undamaged side of the creep's face as his faded blue eyes took in the three girls.

"I'm Tad," he told Bess. "Tad Vlachovic."

"We're looking for a guy," Bess quickly said. "He's about your height, with long black hair—"

Tad slowly shook his head. "Haven't seen this Cass." He glanced over his shoulder. "You guys seen him?"

Two more punk types stepped into the light on the other side of the girls. One was big and burly, with piggy little eyes and a big lower lip that hung down. The other was a skinnier version of Tad, with zits all over his face. "Huh-uh, Tad," Zit-face said.

"Guess you're out of luck with old Cass." Tad's lips twisted more as he looked at Nancy. "But if you're just looking for guys, hey, there's three of you and three of us."

"Sorry, we really have to find our friend," Nancy said firmly. She glanced around. The side street was dark and empty. Tad blocked the way to Janocek Avenue, where there were probably still people on the sidewalks. His assistant creeps blocked the way back to the club—or to Egon's, which was even farther down the block behind them.

Which way?

Nancy decided it would be easier to deal with one creep instead of three. She started toward Janocek Avenue, hoping George and Bess would know what to do.

Tad stepped into her path. "Hey, forget this Cass bozo," he said. "We're giving you three for the price of one."

Nancy stepped around him, but Tad grabbed her arm.

In one swift motion, Nancy shook herself free before he could get a solid grip.

"Ooh," Tad said, his scarred lip twitching. "A feisty one."

Nancy glanced at her friends and then at the better-lit main drag. If George could get Bess moving toward the avenue, she could distract the three creeps until her friends came back with help. George seemed to get the message.

She grabbed Bess's arm and darted down the street as Nancy backed away more slowly, still facing Tad. Mouth-breather and Zit-face took a slow step forward. They needed Tad to tell them what to do.

Tad, however, seemed unconcerned about George and Bess's escape. He had eyes only for Nancy Drew. "Come on, baby," he crooned. "Don't be that way."

His hand flashed out to grab for her again.

This time, Nancy let him catch hold of her arm, just above the elbow. Tad grabbed hard and yanked, obviously expecting her to try to pull away.

Nancy didn't do what he expected. Instead, she stepped forward, pushing in the direction of Tad's pull. It was an old martial arts trick, called moving with the enemy.

Tad quickly found himself stumbling backward. He took a tottering step in an effort to regain his balance.

Nancy didn't let him. With a twist, she freed herself from his clutching hand. She swung around, her arm catching him hard in the chest as her foot swept in behind his ankle.

Tad hadn't seen it coming. One second, he was grabbing the girl. The next, the girl had sent him toppling to the sidewalk on his behind.

He landed hard.

Nancy backed up again, hoping to run off to join her friends. She continued to keep an eye on Tad and his goons.

That should do it, she thought. He won't want to embarrass himself again.

"Think you're smart?" Tad growled.

"Hey, I'm not the one sitting on the pavement," Nancy replied, putting more distance between them.

The two assistant punks took a step forward.

"Oh, got to bring in the reinforcements to handle me?" Nancy taunted.

Tad waved his friends back and rose to his feet. He moved slowly toward Nancy, his hands closing into fists.

Nancy risked a quick glance at the street behind her. Bess and George still hadn't reached Janocek Avenue. It wouldn't do any good to run if there wasn't any help coming yet.

"Hey," Nancy said, backing up more quickly as Tad came on. "I thought you liked feisty girls."

"There's a difference between feisty and stupid," Tad replied. He wasn't smirking now. His upper lip was drawn back in a snarl as he raised his fists.

Chapter

Four

GLAD TO SEE YOU again, Chief," Frank Hardy said as he shook hands with Chief McGinnis of the River Heights Police. Frank was tired and stiff from the day's travel—Bayport to New York, a plane ride to Chicago, and then the drive to River Heights. Night had fallen by the time he and Joe and Chuck Bascomb reached the local police headquarters.

"Your call said this was urgent," Chief McGinnis replied. "I can always make time for something urgent. So can Watch Captain Carter."

The chief was no longer a young man, but he stood straight, and his eyes were pure cop as they took in the Hardys and Chuck Bascomb. Frank thought that the chief looked tired but guessed he still missed nothing. Captain Carter appeared to be a Chief McGinnis in the making, a pedigreed officer.

"This is Chuck Bascomb, an investigator for the State Department," Frank said.

Bascomb produced his battered wallet and ID. "He has reason to believe there might be a political murder about to take place here in River Heights."

The man from the State Department explained that the Rurithenian government had a new business scheme. "The new regime needs money, so it has decided to hire out its former spies to anyone or any country needing an assassin rather than let them come home to become criminals."

"So, you believe a Rurithenian hit man—this Haiduk?—has been hired to kill a target in River Heights?" Chief McGinnis asked.

"We have it from a very good source," Bascomb said. "The problem is, with no solid proof, we can't confront the Rurithenians. Not that I think the secretary of state wants to go public with this, because it would disturb our relations with several of these newly freed states."

Frank and the others stared at the State Department man. "On the other hand," Bascomb added quickly, "we can't allow the Rurithenian Embassy here in the U.S. to set up an organization that other nations can hire to wipe out opponents or enemies. We need to nip this business in the bud."

"Easier said than done," Captain Carter said.

"An assassin always has the advantage over guards. Guards have to be alert twenty-four hours a day. An assassin only has to be successful for a second or two."

The chief looked grim. "From what you're telling me, it sounds as if this Haiduk is a dangerous professional. We'll have to catch him before he gets near the target."

He turned to Bascomb. "We'll need everything you have on the Haiduk. Photos, descriptions, disguises . . ."

The request trailed off when McGinnis noticed Bascomb's embarrassed expression. "We don't know what the Haiduk looks like," he admitted. "We don't even know his or her identity. The Haiduk was a prime intelligence asset—a nondetectable killer. I've already spoken to our intelligence agencies and to the FBI. There's nothing more we can give you other than what I've just told you."

"Worse and worse," McGinnis muttered. "That means we'll have to concentrate our efforts on protecting the prospective victim."

Again, Bascomb shook his head. "I regret to say that we have no idea who the target might be. All we know is that the Haiduk has been hired by one of the former Panaslavan states to eliminate someone in River Heights."

"Panaslava!" the chief repeated in dismay. "We have one of the largest Panaslavan communities right here in River Heights. Little Panaslava is a sizable neighborhood, a town within our town."

"It's a mixed area," Captain Carter put in. "Ritzy stores right next to ramshackle homes. There are lots of immigrants, some who can barely speak English, and both the old-timers and newcomers alike tend to fear anybody in uniform. Some of the newcomers are here illegally—college kids overstaying their student visas, tourists who never went home, not to mention those connected with a smuggling operation coming down from Canada."

He frowned. "When Panaslava was a Communist country, the illegals could claim political asylum here. But you can't become a refugee just because you're afraid of being drafted into a civil war."

"From what I see on television," Frank said, "these wars are destroying cities, leaving people to freeze and starve, and killing thousands of civilians. Those seem to me like very good reasons to flee and become a refugee."

"I agree, Frank. But Captain Carter is approaching the problems of Little Panaslava from a policing point of view. The streets are filled with strangers, people we have no easy way of tracing," Chief McGinnis said. "Still worse, these people come from countries where the police use heavy hands and big clubs. Even the legal residents of Little Panaslava don't trust cops. Our illegal population fears deportation too much to go anywhere near the police—even if it would help stop a murder."

"Great!" Joe Hardy burst out. "We've got a killer no one knows, a target no one knows, and the one thing we're sure of is that the assassin must have a perfect hiding place. What are we supposed to do?"

"We start looking," Bascomb said strongly. Frank was surprised at the resolution in the man's voice. Up to now, Bascomb had struck Frank as mainly apologetic. "We've simply got to fill in the missing pieces and stop the assassination before it happens."

Bascomb focused on Chief McGinnis. "Could you spare us a car and an officer who might know the Little Panaslava area? I'd like to get familiar with the ground as soon as possible."

"Of course," Chief McGinnis replied. But Frank couldn't help noticing that the police officer was a lot less positive than the federal agent.

"Little Panaslava was originally called Little Sarabia. That was back in Teddy Roosevelt's day," Officer Stan Tiso said from behind the wheel of the police cruiser. "And a lot of the buildings and houses still date from that era."

"Do you have a strong landmark protection society here in River Heights?" Chuck Bascomb asked.

Tiso laughed. "I think you might call our policy 'benign neglect.' This was never a happening part of town. It's always been a poor neighborhood. Not a lot of development. If people made money, they moved out to the suburbs or to a different part of town."

"The American dream," Frank muttered.

"That's right." Officer Tiso continued, "For a while, it looked as if Little Panaslava was going to die off. The old folks were the only ones who remembered the old country and the old ways. Then came the new troubles, and with them a new wave of immigrants. All kinds of immigrants—from the well-to-do to the down-and-out. They've breathed a lot of life into the old turf."

"You certainly know a lot about the neighborhood," Joe commented.

Officer Tiso laughed. "Hey, I grew up in Little Panaslava until my dad moved us out—the American dream." The officer nodded at Frank. "Tiso is a fine old Korassian name."

They drove a little farther in silence before Officer Tiso spoke up again. "This street here becomes Janocek Avenue. You could call it the main street of Little Panaslava. We'll cruise around, and I'll introduce you to a couple of contacts. You can start asking about any new people in town."

"We appreciate getting your help," Joe said by way of thanking Officer Tiso.

Frank nodded, but he didn't add the thought that was nagging him: Would that be enough?

When Bascomb finally spoke up, it was to the

Hardys. "Your dossier said you had other, personal local contacts."

Frank nodded. He had called Nancy Drew after they'd arrived in town, but he'd only caught Hannah Gruen—and apparently at a bad time. The Drews' housekeeper had simply said Nancy was out. Frank had promised to try again later.

"I don't know if Nancy and her friends can help much," Joe said. "I've never even heard them mention this part of town. But she is a great detective, so . . ."

They were passing through an area of small factories, auto body shops, and warehouses. It reminded Frank of the run-down harbor area of Bayport before the building boom hit. It may not be pretty, he thought, but those old buildings probably housed the jobs that kept Little Panaslava alive.

Frank noticed that many of the signs weren't in English. He stared at two signs in particular, over the doors to adjacent stores. The signs were written in both Cyrillic and Roman alphabets.

As the police car passed a side street, Frank got a quick glimpse of two girls running through the shadows. They were waving and shouting frantically.

"Stop the car!" he said sharply to Officer Tiso.

"What?" Bascomb said.

The police officer didn't waste time asking questions. He brought the patrol car to a prompt, screeching halt.

Before the vehicle had come to a complete

stop, Frank threw open his door. "Go back down that street we just passed," he told Tiso.

As the officer backed up, Frank ran for the darkened mouth of the side street.

"Hey!" Frank recognized the feminine voice that cried out. "Come back! Police!"

Frank rounded the corner. No, his eyes hadn't been playing tricks. The two girls were Bess Marvin and George Fayne, Nancy Drew's friends.

"Bess, George, what's going on?" Frank asked. "What's the matter?"

Bess just stared at him, her mouth hanging slack in shock.

George was more together. "Nancy . . . down the block . . . trouble . . . three guys . . ."

Frank didn't wait to hear more. "Send the others down," he said, taking off along the side street.

An old-fashioned street lamp cast a pale circle of yellow light around four people in the middle of the block. One of them was female, with reddish blond hair brushing her shoulders. Even with her back to him, Frank immediately recognized Nancy. The other three he didn't know— and he didn't want to know them. They had street punk written all over them.

The three punks were facing off against Nancy. Frank knew that Nancy practiced martial arts, but the odds were definitely against her.

The leader of the pack was advancing on Nancy just as Frank got into yelling range. "Back off!" he shouted, his voice strained from running.

The blond punk turned from Nancy to Frank.

"It must be the famous Cass," he spat out. "We've all been waiting for you."

"I don't know what you're talking about," Frank replied. "But I do know you're about to be in big trouble."

The blond guy sneered. "Yeah? Trouble is my middle name."

Oh, brother, Frank thought. A comic, too.

The jerk waved his friends forward to take Frank. All motion stopped, though, as the *whoop* of a siren cut through the air.

Frank risked a glance away from the attackers to watch Officer Tiso bring the police cruiser barreling down the street.

The big, bulky punk and his skinny sidekick whipped around and fled down an alleyway. The blond one seemed mesmerized by the headlights of the police car. Like a scared rabbit or deer, he didn't move.

Officer Tiso got out, his hand on the butt of his pistol. Joe and Bascomb also exited the vehicle, backing him up. "Well, if it isn't my old pal, Tadeusz Vlachovic," the police officer said, strolling up next to the punk.

"It's Tad," the young guy snapped.

"Sure, *Tad,*" the officer said. "What were you doing here? Making new friends?"

"Hey, these girls were looking for a guy," Tad growled. "Me and my friends offered to help."

"That's why these two girls flagged me down for help, and that's why your friends took off like that." Tiso gave the punk a head rub. "Maybe they've got guilty consciences, huh, Tad?" he said.

"A street gang?" Nancy asked.

Officer Tiso shrugged, as if in apology. "You get all types in Little Panaslava."

"It's a tough neighborhood, Officer," Tad piped up. "I suffer from a bad environment. That's what I'm always hearing at Juvie Court. So, you gonna arrest me, Officer T?"

"That's up to the young ladies." Tiso turned to Nancy. "Do you have a complaint to make, Miss?"

Nancy locked gazes with the blond guy for a long moment. "Not officially," she finally said. "I've got no complaint. Nothing happened."

"It'd be a different story if we hadn't come along," Joe added in a low voice.

"Officer," Bess spoke up. "I'm worried about my friend Cass Carroll. He's a musician. He was playing at a local club earlier this evening. We'd stopped off at the coffee house up the block—"

"Old Egon's?" Tiso said with a smile.

Bess nodded. "Cass went outside, and we haven't seen him since! He's not back at the club. I'm afraid . . ." She glanced at Tad Vlachovic. "I'm afraid that something might have happened to him."

Tiso seemed to expect an explanation from Tad.

"Don't look at me!" Tad protested. "I never saw this Cass guy. Me and the boys were just doing the street when we heard this girl yelling for this Cass. So we checked it out. That's all that happened."

Frank related to Tiso how Tad had called *him* Cass when he'd first come up. It was just possible the punk was telling the truth.

Officer Tiso shrugged. "I don't want to have to see you for a good, long time, *Tadeusz* Vlachovic. Now, get lost." He waved his hand at Tad, and the punk instantly disappeared.

"Maybe you should try to catch your friend at home," the officer suggested to Bess. "And home would be a good place for all you young ladies."

"We've got a car on Janocek Avenue," Nancy said.

As they started off for the car, Nancy hooked arms with Frank.

"Frank and Joe Hardy, our knights in shining armor," she said by way of thanks.

"You know each other?" a surprised Officer Tiso asked.

Frank first introduced Officer Tiso and then Bascomb.

"So, these are your other contacts here?" the government agent asked, surprised.

"Nancy's as good a detective as we are," Joe said defensively.

"I'm sure she is," Bascomb replied, as if Nancy weren't there. He didn't even greet her or the others but turned instead to Officer Tiso. They walked on ahead, deep in conversation.

"He's something else," George said quietly. "Where'd you find him?"

"More to the point," Nancy began, "what are you two doing in River Heights? Not that we aren't glad to see you. As usual, your timing was perfect."

After Frank and Joe told the girls the story of the Haiduk and the threatened assassination, the five friends fell into two smaller groups. Nancy and Frank followed a few paces behind Officer Tiso and Bascomb. Bess, George, and Joe brought up the rear.

"We're going to spend the rest of the evening getting familiar with Little Panaslava," Frank said. "Do you think there's anything you could do to help?"

Nancy shook her head. "I'm just finding out for myself how little I know this neighborhood." She thought for a second. "But Bess's, um, friend lives around here."

"This Cass guy?" Frank asked. "Why do you think he disappeared?"

Nancy shrugged. "We were at this wonderful café—I'll have to introduce you to the owner—when the news broke that the king of Panaslava had been shot in Paris. Most of the people there didn't seem to care one way or another, but Egon—the owner—and another older Panaslavan were quite upset. Then, suddenly, Cass stood up and walked out."

"You think he was upset by the news?" Frank asked.

"I don't think so," Nancy answered. "The younger people there and at the club, later, didn't seem fazed one bit by it." She paused. "Maybe Bess is trying just a little too hard with him," she finally said, "and he needed some breathing space."

They reached Janocek Avenue and paused to let a slow-moving car pass before crossing to Nancy's car.

"Hey, Bess," Nancy suddenly cried. "Isn't that Cass?"

"Hey, you're right," George said. "That must be the record executive he was supposed to meet."

Frank turned toward the passing car. A slim, intense-looking guy with long, dark hair sat in the passenger seat. He was arguing with the driver, a scared-looking older guy with a pale, round face.

Bess came out of her spell as the car pulled directly in front of them. "Cass! Cass!" she called.

Cass glanced in her direction, and his expression became fierce. He waved at Bess to go away and shouted something at the driver.

"Cass!"

The car zoomed off before Bess could reach it.

Chapter

Five

Nancy woke up late the next morning. "Glad we went to the *early* show at that club," she muttered. She quickly ran a brush through her hair, then pulled on a robe and went downstairs to the kitchen.

Hannah was already washing dishes. "I thought you were going to sleep all day," she said.

Nancy stretched until she heard her back pop. "I was thinking about it," she said. "But that would mean missing one of your delicious breakfasts."

"Flattery will get you everywhere," Hannah acknowledged. "How about some blueberry pancakes?"

"Sounds great to me." Nancy glanced over at

43

the kitchen radio. "Mind if I put on the news and hear what I missed while I was catching Z's?"

"Go ahead." Hannah was already at work on the pancake batter.

Nancy set the dial to the local news station, then went to the refrigerator for a glass of orange juice.

"Here are our main stories at the top of the hour," the announcer said. "A murdered man was discovered in a room at the River View Motel. Police aren't giving out details yet—"

"I don't know what this town is coming to," Hannah said. "We never used to have such dreadful crimes—"

Nancy leaned closer to the radio, trying to hear the story. But the station had no more details.

"Nancy Drew," Hannah scolded as she dropped a spoonful of batter onto the hot griddle. "I honestly don't know about you." The hissing sound of Hannah's pancakes cooking was music to Nancy's ears. "Let them report a crime, and you're glued to the radio. If they talk about a body, your eyes start to glow!"

Nancy laughed. "Well," she said, "at least it woke me up. Besides, my eyes don't glow when there's a body."

Still, when she'd finished her stack of blueberry-dotted pancakes, Nancy headed for the living room. Channel 3 news may have more on the killing, she thought. Nancy turned on the television and sat down on the sofa.

The murder was the lead story of the newscast,

and the TV people had indeed gotten more. The murder victim was a man named Pavel Raskol, who was traveling on a diplomatic French passport.

They showed his passport picture, and Nancy leaped up from the couch to stand closer to the TV screen. The picture wasn't very clear, but Nancy did recognize the face. Even in one of those awful ID pictures, he seemed a great deal happier than when she'd last seen him—the night before, arguing in a car with Cass Carroll.

Nancy watched intently but learned nothing more. There was no mention of suspects, and when the broadcast switched to another story, Nancy flicked off the set and flew up the stairs.

After taking a shower and dressing, Nancy headed downtown. She found a parking spot not far from police headquarters and went in.

Maybe I shouldn't be here, she told herself. I could be wrong about having seen the victim with Cass.

But she knew she wasn't. And she wanted to know what else the police had that wasn't on the news. Maybe this could be linked to the murder Frank and Joe were trying to stop.

"Hey, Nancy," a voice called as she moved through the door. She turned to find Frank Hardy beckoning to her. "I wondered when you were going to show up."

"Any progress on your Haiduk case?" Nancy didn't want to ask outright whether they thought Raskol had been the Haiduk's victim.

"None." Frank's welcoming smile flattened. "Unless you count this motel murder as a development."

Nancy looked at him apologetically. "Is it your hit?"

"The man who was murdered—Raskol—was a foreigner, traveling on a French diplomatic passport."

"And we thought he was some kind of record label executive," Nancy said.

"I remember George's saying that," Frank said. "But we still don't know who this Raskol really was. He could have been a French record producer for all we know—"

The two young detectives looked each other in the eye and said in unison, "But I don't think so."

Neither of them had much heart to laugh over their parallel thinking.

"Is Cass's band really that good?" Frank asked.

"Incognito?" Nancy said. "Yes. They are probably that good. Even so, I can't imagine a record producer coming over from Europe to sign them up."

"Well, it would sure beat Joe's theory," Frank said.

"Hey, hey," Joe Hardy complained as he came from the inner recesses of the stationhouse. "Don't go dumping on my idea until Nancy hears it."

"So, tell me, Joe. What's your theory?" Nancy asked.

"Let's just think for a moment," Joe suggested. "Why are Frank and I—and Bascomb—here in River Heights? We're looking for a foreigner—"

"A Rurithenian," Frank interrupted.

"A *foreigner*," Joe continued, ignoring his brother, "who travels around killing people but is shielded by diplomatic immunity. Here we have a dead guy who's a foreigner, with a diplomatic passport—"

"You think Pavel Raskol is the Haiduk?" Nancy asked.

"You don't have to sound so skeptical," Joe said.

"At least Nancy's more polite than Bascomb," Frank pointed out with a grin.

"What do those government bozos know, anyway?" Joe growled.

"Remember, brother, how many times Dad has worked as a government bozo. And I think he would know the difference between a French and a Rurithenian passport," Frank said.

"Cheap shot, Frank," Joe retorted. "But what's the big deal about the French passport? The guy's supposed to be a spy, right? Haven't you ever heard of something called a cover story?"

"I can't think of any cover story that would explain what Raskol was doing with Cass Carroll," Nancy said.

"Maybe they were working together," Joe suggested. "Scouting out River Heights, getting a bead on the target."

"In that case, he certainly didn't do a good job," Frank told Joe. "If I go along with your theory that Raskol was the Haiduk, that means *he* got zipped by whomever he was supposed to kill."

Joe shrugged. "So, maybe Carroll *did* foul up. According to you, the two of them were arguing in the car."

"What I saw was Carroll yelling at Raskol. Not exactly the smartest thing to do with a top-notch assassin," Frank said. "Or even a record producer who's interested in your band."

He turned to Nancy. "What do you think?"

Nancy tried to remember every detail of her lightning-fast glance into the passing car. Cass Carroll had been sitting in the front passenger seat, the expression on his face furious. Raskol was behind the wheel, his face chalky white and sweaty. He had the expression of a frightened man.

Pavel Raskol hadn't looked like a hired killer. Of course, that might be an advantage in the assassin business.

Nancy concentrated harder. The car windows had been closed, so she couldn't hear what the two men were saying. But it was obvious Cass was speaking harshly to Raskol. Nancy was pretty sure Cass was the guy in charge in that car.

That raised all sorts of new questions, such as

what Cass was doing in Raskol's car. If the foreign visitor wasn't a record agent or a hired assassin, what had brought him to River Heights and Cass Carroll?

"Do we know any reason why Raskol might have come to River Heights?" Nancy asked. "Was there anything in his room?"

"Nothing much," Joe said. "He apparently flew into Chicago with just the clothes on his back and a briefcase. He rented a car at O'Hare Airport and drove here. From what we know, we've figured he arrived in Little Panaslava shortly before we did."

"So, probably the first person he contacted was Cass Carroll," Nancy said. "Well?" She stared at the Hardys. "Have the police talked to Cass yet? What does he have to say about all this?"

Frank wouldn't meet Nancy's eyes. "They haven't questioned him yet," he said, almost embarrassed. "Maybe you should talk to Chief McGinnis."

Baffled, Nancy went to the desk sergeant and sent her name back to the chief. A moment later she was walking into the chief's office, a Hardy on either side of her.

What's going on? Nancy wondered. She was getting some very weird vibes from Frank.

Chief McGinnis sat at a desk covered with papers. Standing opposite him was a very tired-looking Officer Tiso, and seated in a chair was a very alert Chuck Bascomb.

"Well, Nancy," the chief said, rising. "It seems

you actually got a glimpse of our murder victim last night."

"I guess I did," Nancy admitted. "Just for a moment. I just heard Joe's interesting theory on his secret identity."

Bascomb dismissed Joe and his theory with a shake of his head. "I think he's been watching too many spy movies."

"We're actually more interested in the car's passenger right now," Chief McGinnis went on. "I understand you've met him."

Nancy nodded. "He's a friend of a friend. I was introduced to him last night at the club where he was playing."

"So you don't know where he lives or where he might hang out in town?" Chief McGinnis pressed.

Nancy glanced around the room. This was beginning to sound like the interrogation of a potentially hostile witness. "As I said, I just met the guy last night. What's going on, Chief?"

"Did you notice any identifying marks?" Chief McGinnis continued. "How was he dressed?"

"Cass has long black hair, gray eyes, and a handsome face with regular features," Nancy replied, trying to keep her temper. "He wore jeans and a flannel shirt and a red hooded sweatshirt. It zipped up the front."

"Sneakers? Shoes?" the chief asked.

Nancy shook her head. "No. He wore big, black, clunky boots. Motorcycle boots. You know, the ones that make your feet look like Frankenstein's monster's feet."

"I don't suppose you noticed any pattern on the soles," Chief McGinnis said.

"It wasn't exactly the first thing I asked him about, no," Nancy replied sarcastically. "What's this all about?"

Chief McGinnis sighed. "You know the routine, Nancy. Raskol was found dead this morning, and the last person he was seen with was Cass Carroll."

Nancy gasped. "Just because we saw the two of them in that car—"

"After we found the body, we questioned all the guests at the motel," Chief McGinnis interrupted. "One of them saw Raskol entering his room with another man. The description he gave matches that of Cass Carroll."

He picked up a pile of photographs and flipped through them, allowing Nancy to see only the backs. "Crime scene pictures," he said curtly. McGinnis pulled one out of the pile and held it out to Nancy.

It was a close-up of a light gray carpeted floor. Just the sort that a motel might have. To one side was a large, wet, reddish brown stain. Blood, Nancy registered.

Beyond the stain, in the middle of the picture, was a footprint. It looked as if the killer had tracked blood after himself as he ran from the murder. A foot-long ruler lay beside the print to give an idea of scale.

Nancy kept staring at the imprint on the rug. It was oversize, the sort of mark a big and clunky boot might make. A motorcycle boot, maybe.

She closed her eyes, feeling sick.

Thanks to her comment, Bess's boyfriend had just become the prime suspect in a murder investigation.

Chapter

Six

Nancy could have kicked herself. What had she just done to Cass Carroll?

She felt a gentle hand on her elbow. "You okay?" Frank Hardy asked. The Hardys and Nancy were still inside McGinnis's office along with Tiso and Bascomb.

Nancy's eyes popped open, and she shook Frank's hand away. He should have told her that Cass was being considered a suspect!

"Oh, I'm just fine," she said tartly, unable to conceal her anger. "Thanks for warning me, *friend.*"

They'd all played her just right, suckering out the information they wanted.

"I *couldn't* tell you," Frank said miserably. "The chief basically ordered us to keep quiet about Cass being under suspicion. He wanted a shot at you with his questions first."

"Well, I'm afraid there's nothing else I can tell you about Cass Carroll, Chief," Nancy said. "All together, I don't suppose we talked for more than half an hour."

"I got some additional information from Egon Marek," Officer Tiso spoke up.

"Who?" Nancy asked.

"Old Egon from the coffee house," Tiso explained. "You mentioned that you had gone there. Mr. Marek was not his usual chatty self. Apparently, Carroll spends time in the café, and Egon has become fond of him. But he finally gave up Carroll's address. It's a boardinghouse near the factory district, the low-rent section of Little Panaslava." He shrugged. "It's a pretty rough area."

So, obviously, someone who lived there would be the one to kill Raskol, Nancy thought sarcastically.

Chief McGinnis stepped around his desk. "Well, I suppose we should pay a visit to Mr. Carroll—if he's come home. Maybe we'll stop by and pick up a search warrant in case he's not."

It was obvious the chief thought that Cass wouldn't be in.

"Could we come along?" Joe asked.

Of course, Joe would like to check out how the River Heights force conducted a search.

But Frank nodded as well, and even Chuck Bascomb added his two cents. "I'll still take all the time I can to case the neighborhood. I'm not convinced that young Mr. Hardy's theory is strong enough to change our tactics."

Frank turned to Nancy. "Coming?"

Nancy just shook her head and walked out of the office. She was still plenty peeved with the Hardys for tricking her.

Besides, she had her own work ahead of her, like breaking the news about Cass to Bess and going over to Dedya Egon's and apologizing for getting him involved.

Nancy walked slowly out of police headquarters and got into her car. Frank didn't bother to catch up.

She jammed the key in the ignition, started the car, and took off toward Bess's.

The neighborhood where the Marvins lived was quiet and pretty, not that far from Nancy's house. Trees lined the streets, rising tall, their branches blending together to create an archway over the road.

Nancy brought her car to a stop in front of the large, neat house. She headed up the walk to the front door and rang the bell.

Mrs. Marvin answered and smiled when she saw who it was. "Nancy!" she said. "Did you forget your workout stuff?"

"Workout stuff?" Nancy repeated.

"Bess called you and George, looking for a workout buddy," Mrs. Marvin explained.

"She must have just missed me." Nancy bit her lip. Did Mrs. Marvin know that Bess was going out with Cass Carroll? Even if she did, knowing that he was a murder suspect would make her pretty frantic.

Nancy walked toward the living room, following the sound of bouncy rock music.

"Five, six, seven, eight!" A chirpy voice counted off in time to the music.

"All right," the cheerful voice went on. "Now we'll go for leg thrusts. You'll need a chair for these—"

Nancy walked into the room to find Bess placing a kitchen chair in front of the television. An aerobic workout video was playing.

"Hey, Nan!" Bess grinned, her face pink from exertion. "I tried to catch you before. Decided to stick a real killer tape in the VCR. I could use a partner."

Bess's hair was pulled back, and she wore a sloppy sweatshirt over clashing baggy sweatpants. For Bess, this was a serious exercise outfit. Her usual aerobics gear ran toward tights and leotards. But that was just for show, especially if there were boys around.

Nancy sighed unhappily. Easygoing Bess always dragged out her exercise tapes when she was feeling anxious about her love life. It looked as though Cass's disappearance the night before had made Bess want to work to make herself prettier, as if she needed any improvement.

"Bess—" Nancy began.

"Want to join me?" Bess asked, her voice bright. "I'm sure I've got something you could wear." She brushed off her sweatshirt. "Something a little better than this."

"We have to talk—about Cass."

Bess shook her head. "I'm not doing this because of Cass. I just need something to get my blood going." Her voice lowered. "That running last night wore me out."

"Bess, this is important," Nancy said.

On the screen, the pretty young girl in the yellow leotard had just finished demonstrating the stretching exercise. Both Bess and Nancy had seen this tape dozens of times. The serious workout was just about to begin.

"Ooh! They're starting!" Bess said. She rested her hands on the back of the chair and raised her leg.

"Bess! Listen to me!" The loud music almost drowned out Nancy's fierce voice as she yanked the chair away from Bess's hands.

Bess stumbled for a second, staring at her friend. "What is it?"

Nancy swallowed and lowered the volume on the TV. It would be better to get right to the point, she decided. "Remember that guy we saw with Cass in the car last night? Well, he was found dead in his motel room this morning. And the last person he was seen with was Cass. They were at the motel together."

Bess's pink face went white. Her jaw fell open, and her eyes widened in shock. "That's crazy!" she insisted.

"The police don't think so," Nancy told her

friend. "They're out looking for Cass. And when I left headquarters, they were getting a search warrant to go over his place."

"They won't find anything," Bess said fiercely. "I've been there." Bess smiled. "It's just a plain rented room—a bed, a closet, and a footlocker. It's just a place for Cass to sleep, hang his clothes, and leave his guitar. The stuff that's really important is hidden—"

Bess gasped, biting off her words.

Nancy shook her head. "Too late, Bess. You blew it."

Bess clamped her lips together and turned away.

Nancy grabbed her friend by the arm and swung her around. "Come on. You can't pretend you didn't say what you said. What is Cass hiding, and where?"

Bess's eyes filled with tears. "It's not—I didn't . . ."

"Cass is in big trouble, Bess. We won't be able to clear him if you go on keeping secrets. Just start from the beginning, and we'll go from there."

Bess glared at Nancy and smeared the sleeve of her shirt across her eyes. "I don't know what Cass is hiding. It's like I told you before, he's a man of mystery. So I did what you always do when you find a mystery. I, I . . ."

"Snooped?" Nancy suggested.

"I decided maybe I should keep an eye on him," Bess corrected. "That's how I know he's not going out with any other girls, or stuff like that. Anyway, while I was checking up on Cass, I saw his hiding place, that's all."

"That's not all, Bess," Nancy said. "Where is it?"

Bess clamped her lips tight, stubbornly setting her jaw. "I don't know," she said.

"Please don't lie to me, Bess," Nancy said. "You've told me this much, you might as well let go of the rest."

Bess shrugged. "It's an alley somewhere in Little Panaslava. I was following him. It's not like I had time to draw a map. Anyway, Cass walked down this alley that goes nowhere. There's this old brick building at the end. Cass dug out a couple of bricks. I guess they must have been loose. Then he pulled out a thin metal box. You know, the kind used in safety-deposit vaults in the bank. He put something in the box, stuck it back in the wall, and left. I got out of there before he saw me."

"Bess, we've got to go there and take a look."

Nancy sighed as her friend again denied what obviously had to be done. "Bess, I know you like Cass. But doesn't that story you just told seem a little strange? Maybe I'd just shrug and say the guy has some funny ideas about privacy, *if* he wasn't now a suspect in a murder."

"He couldn't have killed that guy!" Bess blurted.

"I'm not saying he's the killer. I'm saying we don't know much about Cass Carroll. If we're going to try to help him, we've got to learn more about him. And it seems the only way we're going to find out anything is if we take a look in that box."

She stared at her friend, long and hard. "Now, do you think you can find that alley?"

Bess looked at the carpet, her shoulders slumped. "I think so."

"Then get a coat. We're going—now."

Bess tried to resist as Nancy pushed at her. "Now? Dressed like this?"

"Sure. I'd say you were dressed perfectly for scouting around in an alley," Nancy said. "And the sooner we get there, the sooner we'll be done."

Nancy drove as Bess guided her into a section of Little Panaslava. It wasn't like the shopping area on Janocek Avenue. There were no boutiques or restaurants. The area was shabbier, the streets almost deserted.

"There's Cass's house," Bess said as they passed a ramshackle old wooden house with peeling paint. Three River Heights police cars were parked in front.

"He went down a block here and made a left," Bess directed. For the next couple of minutes, Nancy zigzagged through side streets as her friend tried to remember Cass's route. Twice Bess got them lost. Nancy circled around until they got back on track.

"That's it," Bess suddenly said. She pointed to

an alleyway between a pair of abandoned buildings. A pile of green plastic garbage bags almost blocked the way in.

Nancy peered into the shadows. "Is that the place?" she asked, pointing to a brick wall that angled across her view.

"No. It makes a turn. There's a sort of loading dock. Cass climbed up onto it."

Nancy led Bess into the alleyway. The wall she'd seen wasn't the end. The passage angled off to the left.

"I peeked around the corner from here to watch him," Bess whispered. "I guess that's why he never spotted me."

Nancy turned the corner and faced the rear of what had once been a factory or warehouse. Huge iron shutters hung drunkenly on rusted hinges. The glass was gone from all the windows. Nancy began to see the sense in using this wreck of a building as a hiding place. Probably no one had been in it in years.

She climbed onto the ruins of a loading dock, then helped pull Bess up after her.

Well, I have to give Cass Carroll credit for having guts, Nancy thought. I'd be afraid this wall would fall on me. Up close, she could see several places where the mortar that had held the bricks together had disappeared entirely.

"Where did Cass start digging?"

"You have to bring that old wooden case over here." Bess pointed to the case leaning against the wall. Nancy moved it to a spot just past one of the yawning window holes. She climbed up and examined several of the bricks, jiggling them with her finger. Yes, they were loose. But it wouldn't be easy getting them out. She looked around on the dock and found a long, thin piece of rusted metal, part of a broken shutter.

Wedging her improvised crowbar into a crack, Nancy shoved and twisted. The bricks began to give. She heaved, and bricks fell thunderously to the ground.

"Cass was quieter," Bess said.

"Cass had more time to waste," Nancy replied. Rising up on her tiptoes, she peered into the hole she'd created. There was a space between the brick outer wall and the plaster inside. Was that a glint of metal?

Carefully poking down through fragments of brick and dust, she found the corner of a long, thin strongbox.

"Got it!" Nancy announced. She jiggled the box loose and pulled it free.

Then she discovered that Cass hadn't just depended on a hiding place to keep his secrets. There was a lock on the treasure chest, an expensive, sturdy kind of lock that couldn't be easily broken or picked.

"We're going to need tools to get this thing open," Nancy said in annoyance. "A hacksaw or something like that."

"No, you won't, babe."

Nancy's head snapped around, and she saw Tad Vlachovic standing below her at the foot of the loading dock. The smirk was back in full force on the guy's scarred face.

"You can just hand it right down here," he said harshly.

Chapter

Seven

NANCY'S BRAIN SHIFTED into high gear. She studied the situation almost as if it were a puzzle or a school assignment. The problem: how to get herself and Bess to her car, which was parked on the street, outside the alley. The obstacle: Tad Vlachovic, standing between them and the only way out. There were two of them and one of him, but Bess wasn't used to fighting. And Tad Vlachovic, unfortunately, seemed as if he'd be rather skilled at it.

Worse, he seemed to read her mind as she stood there on the loading dock, Cass Carroll's treasure box under her arm.

"You don't even want to think about getting cute," Tad warned. "And don't try pulling any of that 'finders keepers' jazz on me. This is my turf." He gestured as if the abandoned buildings were some kind of kingdom. "And whatever turns up on my turf is *mine.*"

As if to back up his point, Tad made a knife suddenly appear in his right hand. "So don't mess around, babe. You and Blondie over there have given me enough trouble already."

Nancy glanced over at Bess, who was standing stock-still, frozen with fear. "All right," Nancy said, defeat sounding in her voice. "You want it, you've got it."

Holding out the metal box, she jumped off the old loading dock.

On the way down, she switched her grip on the box. As she landed, the edge of the heavy metal strongbox landed right on Tad Vlachovic's wrist.

His howl was part pain, part fury. His hand jerked, and the knife dropped to the littered ground. Nancy didn't think she'd broken any bones, but for the next couple of minutes, Tad would be a lefty.

He lunged at her, reaching for the box. His clumsy swipe missed, but Nancy lost her hold on the box, which swung wildly, smashing into the brick loading dock. Nancy grabbed at it, catching it at one end with both hands. Tad came at her again. Nancy swung the long box like a baseball bat. It caught him right in the gut.

Tad folded over but still tried to wrap an arm around the strongbox. Nancy yanked it back and quickly shifted her eyes to Bess, who still hadn't moved.

"Come on!" Nancy yelled.

That woke her up. Bess didn't need a second invitation. At least she was wearing a pair of cross-trainers. She leaped off the loading dock, handling the four-foot fall with only a stumble. Tad tried to go for her, but Nancy smacked him again with the box, throwing him off.

Bess dashed down the alley. A second later Nancy was following her.

Behind her Tad Vlachovic muttered something nasty-sounding in his other language. He didn't waste any more breath as he took off after them.

Nancy caught up with and passed Bess, the long metal box tucked under one arm. Her hand dug in her jeans pocket for her car keys. She rounded the corner of the passageway. Ahead was daylight, almost unnaturally bright after the long shadows of the alley.

With an extra burst of speed, Nancy leaped and cleared the pile of green garbage bags dumped at the alley mouth. She landed awkwardly, nearly falling on her face, but she staggered a bit, got her balance, and caught herself on the hood of her car.

The keys were in her hand, and she unlocked the driver-side door. Dumping Cass's strongbox under the seat, she snaked across the car to unlock the passenger door. Then she jammed the key in the ignition and turned to see how Bess was doing.

Her friend was moving with all the speed of an adrenaline rush. Tad was still a couple of steps behind her as she burst out of the alley, but he was gaining. His big boots pounded the pavement.

Bess darted around the car and hauled on the door as Nancy started the engine. As soon as Bess was inside, and before she could even close the door, Nancy pulled away. The car fishtailed wildly for about half a block. Luckily, there wasn't any other traffic.

In the rearview mirror, Nancy saw Tad Vlachovic shaking his fist. All they'd left for him were a couple of feet of tire tracks.

As soon as they caught their breath, the girls laughed shakily.

"That—was—*not*—the kind of exercise I was looking for today!" Bess declared, still gasping. "When I saw that knife—"

"You and me both," Nancy confessed. "I'm glad you followed my lead."

She took a different route through the maze of side streets back to Janocek Avenue. Now that the excitement had worn off, her hands began to tremble. So much could have gone wrong in those final few seconds.

Still, they'd come out okay. And they had important evidence. Nancy pulled to the side of the road, reached under the seat for the box, and smiled. Bess nodded, as if consenting to Nancy's next move. Feeling safe enough to stop, Nancy pulled over to the curb.

Cass Carroll had gone for the top of the line in locks but not in strongboxes. Getting banged against the bricks had bent the metal loop that held the lock. By using the lock itself as a lever, Nancy was able to twist the weakened metal back and forth until it broke. The lock fell off, and Nancy opened the hinged top.

She stared in surprise. Inside were a number of thin bundles of bills—American dollars and some foreign currency. Several folded papers were held together with rubber bands. With Bess eagerly peering over her shoulder, Nancy opened one bundle, which turned out to be a stack of handwritten letters in a language neither of them knew. Panaslavian?

Another bundle of letters was typed on the letterhead paper of a famous recording company. "At least Cass was being honest with us last night," Nancy said with a glance at Bess. "It looks like Incognito is close to signing a record deal."

"Hey, that's great!" Bess exclaimed. "Let me see."

Instead, Nancy bundled the papers back into the box and slipped it under the seat. Then she started up the car again.

"Ah, come on, Nancy, now that you got the box open, I should at least get a better look."

Bess swiveled around to look out all windows. "Where are we going?" she asked. "You just missed our turnoff."

Nancy had indeed just passed the turn that would take them back to their neighborhood. But that wasn't her destination. She was heading for the business district of River Heights—and police headquarters.

"Nancy, you said we had to take a look at that box. Okay, we couldn't hang around in Little

Panaslava with that creep there. I thought we'd take it to your house, or mine, and then—"

"And then what?" Nancy asked. "Quietly put it back? Tad knows about the hiding place now, Bess. It's not a secret anymore."

"But Cass—"

"I know, Bess," Nancy said sorrowfully. "We've just ripped off Cass's bank account. But what else could we do in the circumstances? We couldn't have guessed that that punk Tad would show up."

"But we don't have to take it to the police," Bess cried. She was obviously getting very upset over this.

Nancy sighed. "It's evidence," she said.

"Evidence of what?" Bess demanded. "When you dragged me out of my house, you only talked about helping Cass, about clearing his name. You didn't say anything about giving his stuff to the cops."

"I still want to help Cass," Nancy said firmly. "But we can't do it by hindering a murder investigation. Holding back evidence is against the law."

"Yeah? Well, ratting out a friend should be, and that's what you're making me do to Cass." Bess reached under the seat and scooped up the box. "Stop the car."

"Bess, be reasonable—" Nancy began.

"I said, *stop the car!*"

Nancy pulled over, but before her friend could get out, Nancy reached over and grabbed Cass Carroll's box.

"Let go!" Bess tried to wrench the box away, but all she managed to do was spill the contents on the floor.

Nancy sighed and began to collect the packets of money and letters that lay scattered at their feet. Abruptly, she stopped. There was something new in the mix—a little booklet in a plastic case.

"What's this?" Nancy asked. When she picked up the plastic case, gummy adhesive stuck to her fingers. "Whatever this is, it must have been taped into the far end of the box, the part beyond the hinged top."

In other words, she thought, it had been hidden.

With Bess watching, Nancy examined the little booklet. The stiff burgundy cover was stamped in gold with a coat of arms. Gold letters appeared below: "République Française."

"French Republic," Nancy murmured. "Bess, it's a French passport." Her mind went back to the news report of Pavel Raskol's death. He'd been traveling on a French passport, too.

Tucking the box under her arm, Nancy took out the passport. It was made out to a Casimir Karolyi, and the thin, proud, handsome face in the passport photograph was definitely that of Cass Carroll.

Chapter

Eight

Nancy closed the passport with a snap. "Okay, Bess, this does it. We've *got* to turn this stuff in to the police."

"Why?" Bess stubbornly demanded.

"Look, the questions about Cass are just multiplying. He's Panaslavan, right? But he has a British accent. He's got a French passport, under a different name, and he was the last person to be seen with a murder victim—who also had a French passport. What is he hiding? Why doesn't he use his real name?"

"He's a musician," Bess countered. "It helps to have a name people can pronounce."

"That's not the way it looks to me," Nancy said unhappily. "I have a feeling Cass is living here illegally."

Bess's voice rose as her face went red. "And

because you think he *may* be an illegal alien, you also think he's a murderer?"

"Bess, you're twisting what I said," Nancy responded. "I'm not saying he *is* a murderer, but how is he going to clear his name by hiding? A man of mystery is fine in a romance, but this is real life, Bess."

"I can't believe you're talking this way." Bess shook her head.

That really set Nancy off. "Bess Marvin, wake up! Like it or not, your boyfriend is mixed up in a murder."

Bess gazed steadily at Nancy. "I want you to give me that box."

Nancy sighed. "I can't, Bess." She started the car. "Cass is a fugitive. I have to help the police find him."

"I trust Cass," Bess insisted. "I thought I could trust you, too. Give me his box."

Nancy stopped at a red light. "No, Bess. I'm sorry."

"Great!" Bess said, her voice quavering with unshed tears. "That's just great. I don't think we have anything more to say, then—ever."

She flung open the door, slammed it shut behind her, and stomped off down the street.

Nancy stared after her friend until the car behind her honked its horn. The light had turned green. Should she go after Bess?

The strongbox on Nancy's lap seemed to weigh a ton. She stepped on the gas.

* * *

The box sat on Chief McGinnis's desk, its top open. Using an oversize pair of tweezers, the chief took out each item while another officer made a list.

"Three hundred forty dollars in small bills, approximately the same amount in French francs." The tweezers drew out a flat plastic wallet. "Traveler's checks, made out to Casimir Karolyi. Hundred-dollar denominations—I'd say there's a good five thousand dollars in here."

He glanced at Nancy. "Pretty well-off for a guy who lived one step up from a flophouse."

"He might have been better off yet," Nancy said. "Some of the letters in there talk about a recording contract for his band."

"It's all very interesting," McGinnis said. "But there's nothing here to tie Carroll in with the late Mr. Raskol—unless we find something when we translate those letters."

Nancy wanted to put in a good word, for Bess's sake. "I've met Cass. I don't really think he is a killer. A little mysterious . . ."

"Based on half an hour's conversation in a club and a café," Chief McGinnis countered.

"Bess Marvin has known him longer. She's convinced he's innocent."

"Pardon me," Chief McGinnis said, "but girl-friends aren't always the best judges of some-one's guilt or innocence."

Nancy nodded. "But all you really have is that footprint at the murder scene. Lots of people wear motorcycle boots."

"Look," said the chief. "I'm not after Cass Carroll because I dislike the young man, Nancy. I want him for questioning. He was the last person seen with Pavel Raskol."

Nancy nodded, feeling rather miserable. Then an idea struck her. "Chief, I'd like to talk to the other guys in the band."

"Are you implying that my investigators didn't do a thorough job?" he asked teasingly.

Nancy shrugged apologetically. "It's just that these guys might open up a bit more with someone their own age."

"Don't rub it in." The chief chuckled at his little joke. "Officer Tiso will give you the addresses. Just let us know if you turn up anything interesting."

Maybe if I can get to the bottom of this, Bess will forgive me—as long as Cass isn't the murderer, Nancy thought as she left the chief's office.

Nancy saw Officer Tiso talking with Frank and Joe Hardy in the outer office. "We tracked down Carroll's day job," he was saying, "from some pay stubs in his rented room."

"So chances are he's here legally," Joe piped up. "If he's on the payroll . . ."

"Well, that's good news," Nancy said. "The chief sent me to you for the addresses of the other musicians in Incognito. I'm going to go talk to them." Nancy turned to the Hardys. "Want to come?"

Frank shrugged. "Sure. We'd probably get further on our case hanging out in Little Panaslava than here."

But as it turned out, Danilo Slovic, the drummer and first on the list, lived with his folks in a quiet neighborhood outside Little Panaslava.

The house wasn't hard to find. Music blared from the garage. The door was wide open, and they could see three musicians inside.

Nancy winced. Was this Incognito? They sounded awful.

As Nancy and the Hardys got out of the Hardys' car and headed up the driveway, the noise stopped. Milek, the keyboardist, now on bass, was yelling. "Gavi, you're playing that guitar like you're wearing a baseball glove!"

"It's my first time playing the lead!" the lanky, dark-haired guitarist shouted back. "Cass always—" Then he noticed Nancy. "Hey, there. Danilo, introduce your friend."

The blond-haired drummer stared at Nancy in confusion. "I don't— Wait, you were with Cass and Bess last night."

"Right," Nancy said. "I'm Nancy Drew. These are my friends, Frank and Joe Hardy. And you're Danilo Slovic?"

The drummer nodded. "That's Milek Bledny on bass, and that's Gavi Nektar *trying* to play lead guitar."

"I'm the *bass* player!" Gavi complained. "Is it my fault that I don't know Cass's part, too? Besides, who died and left you boss?"

The sound of the word *died* brought a sudden silence to the members of Incognito.

"We know that the police want to talk to Cass," Danilo said. "We don't know where he is. We told them what we know."

"Which isn't much," Milek offered.

Gavi picked up the thread. "Cass disappeared after our first set last night, and we haven't seen or heard from him since."

"What do you think about that?" Nancy asked.

"We don't know what to think," Milek said. "Cass is a nice guy, but he's private. Maybe it's because he's more of an outsider. Danilo and I have known each other for years. We were kids together in summer camp. We met Gavi through a Panaslavan social club about a year ago. That's when we started playing together."

"Danilo is our token American," Gavi said with a grin. "He was born over here. Milek came to this country with his parents years and years ago. I'm living with my aunt and uncle." His smile faded. "I was supposed to be going to university back home, but the trouble started."

"How did you meet Cass?" Frank asked.

"Milek met him in the Seven-Eleven," Gavi said.

"It was about four months ago. I was bringing my keyboard to practice and stopped off to get a soda," Milek said. "Cass asked about the keyboard while he was ringing me up, and he started talking about music. We needed a lead guitar, so—"

"Now he's the leader of the band," Danilo said. "Cass gave us our name, whipped us into shape, and started getting us gigs."

"He had some nerve." Gavi laughed. "He'd get us auditions at clubs I'd never have dared to hit. Club managers didn't scare him." He glanced sourly at Milek. "Unlike some people, who let us get cheated out of more than half our money last night."

"We didn't play for half the night—our lead guitarist walked out, remember?" Milek shot back.

"Had you ever met or seen the man who was killed?" Nancy stepped in to cut off the argument. "Pavel Raskol?"

The members of Incognito shook their heads.

"Cass never mentioned him?" Joe asked.

"Cass never mentioned *anything* about anything," Danilo answered. "All we really knew about him was his taste in music."

"Do you know of any reason why he would be so secretive?" Nancy asked. "Could he have been here illegally?"

The musicians shifted uneasily.

"We didn't ask, and he didn't tell," Danilo finally said.

"I wondered about it," Gavi admitted. "A couple of times I tried to talk to him about home. He acted like he didn't want to hear it."

"So what else can you guys tell me?" Nancy asked.

Danilo shook his head. "Cass is a nice guy. He sings and plays guitar like an angel." He glanced at the other members of the band. "But the more people ask me questions about him, and this murder, the more I realize how little I know about the guy."

"Hey, guys," Nancy said as they got into Frank and Joe's car. "Do you mind swinging by Dedya Egon's café?"

"Hungry, Nancy?" Joe asked with a conspiratorial smile.

"Not in the slightest," Nancy replied. "I just need to talk to him for a minute. I won't be long."

As they pulled up in front of Old Egon's café, Nancy asked Frank and Joe to wait for her in the car.

"You want us to wait *outside* the best café in River Heights?" Joe asked, appalled.

"I'll bring you a doggy bag," Nancy said. "I want to talk to Dedya Egon alone."

Nancy felt very alone as she walked across the street. She had put Chief McGinnis onto Egon in the first place, and the chief had browbeaten him into giving out Cass's address. She knew she had been used, but Dedya Egon didn't.

The café was fairly full as Nancy walked through the door, but Old Egon was by her side before she even had a chance to look for him.

"Mudrashka Natalya," he said quietly. "You are here by yourself? No policemen?"

"Dedya Egon, please," she started.

"No, we will not talk here," Old Egon said. "Come with me." He took Nancy's arm and led her through the kitchen to a back room that was furnished as a little sitting room. On the way, Egon asked one of the kitchen boys to bring them coffee and pastries.

"Please, Natalya, sit down," Egon said. He waited until she was settled on a small love seat before sitting down next to her. A tall young man with close-cropped black hair entered with a tray.

"I'm not here to eat," Nancy began. But Egon raised his hand to quiet her until the man from the kitchen had gone.

"I know you are not here to eat, but talk is always better with food."

"Dedya Egon, I want to apologize." Nancy took the cup and saucer he had extended to her. "If I hadn't told the police I'd been here—"

"But you were here, Natalya," Dedya Egon interrupted to Nancy's surprise. "And I knew you would be back."

"But I didn't mean to get you involved," Nancy said. "They tricked me. I didn't know they were looking for Cass."

Old Egon sighed. "It is difficult not to tell the police what they want to know. When I was young—a child—the police asked everyone questions, about friends, about family. They had the power to make you tell what you did not want to. But this is not old Panaslava. The police did not beat me. They did not threaten me. They asked me a simple question, and I answered it."

Nancy was confused. "Are you saying you wanted to tell them? But I thought you would want to protect Cass."

"I would be the first to protect Casimir, if he needed it," Dedya Egon said passionately. "But I am an old man, and I have seen truth in the world, and I have seen deception. What good are lies? I have found that truth is a powerful mistress. I think you know that, and you believe in her, too."

Nancy suddenly realized why she had come. It was Bess she was afraid she had betrayed. And Dedya Egon had calmed her fears.

"They are still looking for him," she said.

"Yes, I know." Dedya Egon nodded.

"Do you know where he is?" Nancy asked. "If he's innocent, why is he hiding?"

"I do not know where our friend is," Old Egon answered. "If I did, I would tell him what I have told you. Now, here." He wrapped a handful of miniature tarts and cookies in a napkin. "Put these in your pocket for later."

As he opened the door to the kitchen, the kitchen worker who had served them coffee was standing right outside.

"What? You have no work to do? Do the pastries bake themselves?" Dedya Egon cried with obvious affection in his voice.

The young man ducked his head and hurried back to the ovens.

"You are good to everyone, aren't you, Dedya Egon?" It was more of an observation on Nancy's part than a question.

The old man put his finger to his lips. "Shh," he whispered. "I like them all to think I am an old ogre."

As Nancy crossed the street, Joe rolled down his window. "Did you bring your poor bodyguards a treat?"

Nancy emptied her pockets through the window into Joe's outstretched hands and got into the backseat without a word.

"What did he say?" Frank asked. "Does he know where Cass is?"

"We talked about truth," Nancy said with a smile. "And he doesn't know where Cass is."

"The chief will be thrilled to hear your report," Frank replied.

"Ha," Nancy cried. "I'm not likely to tell him that I was here—again! Dedya Egon did say one thing the chief might like to hear about. He slipped up once. He called Cass 'Casimir.'"

"Sounds like your Dedya Egon knows more of the truth than he's telling," Frank said.

Nancy and the Hardys found Chief McGinnis talking to Officer Tiso outside his office.

"Get anything interesting?" the chief asked hopefully.

"If I hadn't left my car down here, I wouldn't have bothered to come back," Nancy responded.

Frank shook his head. "I don't think they've got a band without Cass," he said.

"Somehow," the chief said, "I don't think that has much of an impact on the case—"

"Aha!" A cry of satisfaction suddenly arose from the corner of the room. Everyone turned to see Chuck Bascomb removing a piece of paper from the fax machine. "We just got word from my friends at the State Department about Pavel Raskol's diplomatic passport."

"I'm all ears," McGinnis said.

"Raskol was a Panaslavan exile who was living in Paris," Bascomb began. "That explains the French passport."

"And the diplomatic angle?" Nancy asked.

"That, it seems, was courtesy of the French government." Bascomb scanned the fax. "'Diplomatic status is sometimes offered to certain governments in exile,'" he read.

"What?" Nancy said. "I don't understand."

"Pavel Raskol was part of the entourage attached to the Panaslavan throne of the late King Boris!"

Chapter

Nine

Is it me," Joe Hardy asked, "or is this case getting loopier and loopier?"

Nancy was unable to resist. "It's you," she said.

"Ah, now that's the Nancy I know and love," Joe said. "You've been treating me too nicely. I was afraid you'd lost your edge."

The six detectives working the Raskol murder all stood around a desk trying to read the fax that had come in from the State Department. Raskol had been granted a diplomatic French passport as part of King Boris's retinue.

"Didn't you say there was a French passport in that box of Cass's you brought in?" Frank asked Nancy.

She nodded. "But I don't think it was a diplomatic passport. It looked like the plain, ordinary variety—made out to Casimir Karolyi."

"Raskol came from France," Joe said. "He was hanging out there with this exiled King Boris."

"The late King Boris," Nancy added. "He was assassinated."

"So," Frank said, "the king is killed in France. And within a day or two, his—what? courtier? henchman?—is killed here in River Heights."

"All of a sudden, this case seems to be taking a new and very political turn," Joe said with a frown.

"You mean you're giving up the theory of Raskol being the Haiduk?" Nancy teased.

Joe shrugged, rereading the fax. "According to his passport, Raskol didn't leave Paris all year, but Bascomb said that the Haiduk made three hits during that time."

Agent Bascomb frowned at Joe. "None of which was in France," he added.

"You see?" Joe said, as if *he* were talking Nancy out of the theory that Raskol was the Haiduk. "Now, Casimir—that sounds like a foreign name. Could *he* be the Haiduk?"

"Hello, Joe," Frank called. "We know Cass Carroll has been here in River Heights for at least four months. And the Haiduk's last hit was three months ago, right, Bascomb?"

"So the State Department thinks," Bascomb muttered.

"Cass is a little young to be a Cold War spy, anyway, Joe," Nancy argued. "For Cass to be the

Haiduk, he'd have to have started his career when he was about ten years old."

"Ah, the perfect cover! Who would expect a child to be an assassin?" Joe glanced around at the unsmiling faces. "That was a joke, folks."

"It wasn't funny," Frank replied. "I'll just point out one more problem with your theory. Cass has been in River Heights for four months. If he was sent here to kill someone, don't you think he'd have done it before now?"

"Maybe someone *was* killed, only we don't know it," Joe suggested. Everyone looked at him as if he'd gone crazy.

"Earth to Joe," his brother said quietly. "Someone *was* killed—Raskol."

"Look," Nancy spoke up, a tone of finality in her voice, "we've got two people from Eastern Europe who live in France. One is dead, and we're hypothesizing that the other is the murderer. Right?" She didn't wait for an answer. "Why go to all the trouble of arranging for one to murder the other in America? Why not do it in France? Paris has dark alleys, too."

"I think it all comes down to what Raskol was doing in America in the first place." Bascomb leaned forward in his chair, apparently ready to give his opinion. "And specifically, why he came to River Heights."

"Okay, I'll bite," Joe said. "Why?"

"In a word, money," Bascomb replied. "There's a big Panaslavan community in this town. The immigrants here, even the Panaslav-

Americans, probably have relatives or friends in the various factions back home. Those factions need guns and other supplies, and you can be sure they've been trying to raise funds for them here, in America."

Bascomb sat back again. "We know that Raskol was traveling light."

"Just the clothes on his back and a briefcase," Joe said.

"And the cops haven't been able to find the briefcase," Frank added.

Bascomb nodded. "Not surprising if the briefcase was filled with money."

"That would explain—" Nancy began, then abruptly stopped.

Joe looked at her. "Explain what?"

Nancy cleared her throat. "It might explain why Cass didn't go for the money he had stashed away," she said in a low voice.

Bascomb nodded. "Exactly. He wouldn't need money if he'd already hijacked some other funds. It could even explain why he was hanging around town. He was waiting for Raskol to show up."

Joe took in the unhappy expression on Nancy's face and seemed to read her thoughts. "Bess won't want to hear this," he said.

"The mayor's given the okay for overtime," Chief McGinnis announced. "Tiso, call in all of our off-duty people. We're doing a house-to-house search through Little Panaslava."

Janocek Avenue was a little drab in daylight

without the bright neon signs in the shop windows. Chuck Bascomb had stayed behind, saying he had reports to send to Washington, but Joe, Frank, and Nancy were on the scene.

Word of the impending house-to-house search had raced through the community. As the Hardys and Nancy arrived at Chief McGinnis's improvised command post, so did a delegation of local merchants. One of them, a tall, distinguished-looking older man with silver-white hair, peered at Nancy.

"Mudrashka Natalya!" the man exclaimed as if they hadn't seen each other in a very long time.

"Dedya Egon!" Nancy replied, sounding just as surprised.

Officer Tiso's surprise was legitimate. "You know each other? Mr. Marek is an important man in this community, Nancy. Some people call him the unofficial mayor of Little Panaslava." He looked at her suspiciously. "I thought you said you were unfamiliar with Little Panaslava."

Before Nancy could answer, the elderly gentleman scoffed. "Ach, if I am so important, perhaps I might have heard a little earlier about all these police coming and going from door to door—acting like they're here to persecute us."

"Please, Mr. Marek," Chief McGinnis began. He sounded embarrassed. "This is not old Panaslava. We're looking for two people—one young man, Cass Carroll." He paused, all embarrassment gone. "Also known as Casimir Karolyi."

If Chief McGinnis hoped to surprise Egon with his knowing Cass's real name, he missed his mark. But his words were not lost on some of the other merchants. A few gasps were uttered but quickly hushed.

"Mr. Carroll is wanted for questioning in the murder investigation of Raskol. The other man, or woman, we are looking for is a terrorist, a hired assassin, known as the Haiduk."

This was a surprise to Old Egon. His face darkened as if thunderclouds had rolled across the clear sky above.

"We hope that you and the local residents will assist us in our search," the chief said. "Especially by explaining the search to your neighbors. We wouldn't want them to imagine anything that isn't true."

"Of course, we will help the police," Egon Marek said, having regained his composure.

The group of merchants murmured their agreement.

"But," Old Egon continued, "I have to go to supervise the baking, so I must return to my establishment."

The group broke up. Chief McGinnis and Officer Tiso headed out with their band of searchers, which included a few merchants who agreed to explain situations or act as translators.

A little while later, Nancy and the Hardys entered Egon's café. Egon smiled at the young people. "You're just what I need!" he said. "The

baking is being finished, now comes the tasting."
He patted the flat midriff of his double-breasted
blazer. "If I want to continue fitting into this
jacket, I need volunteers to taste.

"Sit, sit," Egon commanded. "Take a break
while I collect some samples." He disappeared
into the kitchen before they could respond.

Joe turned to Frank, who Joe knew was impa-
tient to continue the search. "Just think what we
may find out from Little Panaslava's unofficial
leader," he pointed out to quiet Frank.

"Hmm," Frank said skeptically. "I have a
feeling you're only talking with your stomach."

Egon reappeared with a tray of coffee and
delicious-looking pastries. Joe's mouth began to
water.

Before Joe could even take his first bite, the
bell over the door jangled, and in walked Officer
Tiso.

"Officer Tiso," Egon called. "Could I tempt
you to join us?"

The police officer shook his head. "I'm sorry,
Egon, but the chief assigned me to check your
café."

"So, the hunt is on." The older man stepped to
the next table and twitched away the tablecloth.
"Will this convince you I have no one hiding
under the tables?"

Tiso sighed. "You know I have to search, Egon.
You're a special friend of Cass Carroll's."

"All right," Egon said. "Nancy, boys, start
eating! My pastries are best when they're warm."

Joe could hear the two men's footsteps recede as Old Egon took the officer on a tour of the premises—the kitchen, storerooms, office, and basement.

"No fugitives, eh?" Egon said as he escorted Tiso to the door. "Now may I chat with my guests?"

Returning to their table, the café owner asked, "How did you like everything?"

Joe smiled. "It was delicious!"

"Good!" Egon laughed. "That's what I like to hear."

Frank nodded his agreement. "Do you mind if we ask you a few questions ourselves?" he asked the older man.

Egon smiled. "Little Panaslava has never received such attention before. I wish the circumstances were different, but I am always glad to talk. Go ahead, ask."

"You know a lot about what happens in the neighborhood," Frank said. "Do people here raise money for the various factions back home?"

Egon's smile dimmed a little. "For centuries, Sarabians shoot Korassians, Zelenogorans shoot Albanians, and everybody shoots the Turkish collaborators in Cerce-Kamen! The old people here shake their heads, but the young ones bring the battles from Panaslava to the streets of Little Panaslava. Some give up their money, but not many. And where does it go?" Egon paused, almost as if he expected an answer. "It goes into the pockets of a few rather than the hands of the many."

An awkward silence followed, until Egon began to chuckle. "You did not know that to ask Old Egon a question is to get either a sermon or a history lesson—or both, if you are lucky."

"I'll take my chances with another question," Nancy said. "Why do people call King Boris the pretender to the throne of Panaslava? I don't get it. How can he be king and a pretender at the same time?"

Egon sighed. "The world is a complex place, yes, Natalya? Old King Boris was from the Ladinovic family, who ruled until World War Two. After the war, the big powers shuffled our small countries like a deck of cards and dealt a new hand. The Vlachovics from Sarabia then ruled for a few years until the Communists took over. They ruled with an iron fist, I might add. They decreed the Ladinovics outlaws and hunted them down so they would have no competition for the throne."

"Vlachovics?" Nancy said in surprise. "You mean like Tad Vlachovic?"

Egon's face became sour. "Oh, I know young Tadeusz, and he is far from royal. A troublemaker, that boy." He shook his head. "No, Vlachovic is a common name, like Jackson is over here. In fact, the *vic* in our names is an old Slavic ending, which means 'son of.'"

He paused to drink his coffee before continuing with his history lesson. "When the Communists came, the Vlachovic royal family was all killed, but old Boris Ladinovic, who had been in hiding in the mountains of Zelenogora, managed to rescue the royal regalia—the jewels and gold that meant kingship to our many people. He escaped with them. So, he and his descendants are now our kings. To some, however, he was a pretender because he was not a Vlachovic."

"Fascinating," Frank said.

"So, whoever has the royal regalia is the king?" Nancy asked.

"More or less," Egon answered. "But there is always more than one way to be the ruler of any country."

Just then Joe found his mouth stretching in a yawn he couldn't hide. "Sorry about that," he apologized. "It's not the company, I promise you."

"No wonder you fall asleep. You listen to an old man talk of things that happened long before you were born," Egon said. "It doesn't help that you are full of good pastry and sitting in a nice, warm shop."

"Maybe we should get moving," Joe admitted.

Egon accompanied them to the door, waving away offers of payment. "That was just to taste. Come again another time. You may pay then."

The café owner opened his door just in time for a tall, elegant older woman to stride in. "Madame Strulenka!"

Joe stared, not at the woman, though she was

striking, but at Old Egon. The guy actually bowed from the waist and clicked his heels.

"May I present Madame—excuse me—the Grofina Strulenka. These are my young friends, Nancy Drew and Frank and Joe Hardy." He turned to the trio and said, "Madame Strulenka is a countess of old Panaslava."

The countess nodded her head in greeting.

"Madame is also a generous landlady." Egon gestured to a huge, old-fashioned house across the street. "She turned her home into a hostel for visiting university students."

Madame Strulenka appeared to be a little embarrassed. "I have plenty of room."

"And our countrymen have a great need," Egon said. "If those fools at home have their way, a whole generation of young people will be cheated out of educations while civil wars rage. This way, some at least will be free to learn."

"How very gallant, Egon." The lady smiled. "But . . ."

"A thousand pardons," Egon apologized. "I am keeping you from speaking."

Madame Strulenka's smile dimmed a little. "I just heard that the police were coming into all the houses. I am afraid they might frighten some of the newly arrived students. . . ."

She was too late. Shouts rang out from her house across the street. Egon and his guests stepped out of the café just as the attic window in Madame Strulenka's house shattered.

A moment later a young man appeared in the opening. He was tall and slim. Joe caught a glimpse of long, dark hair as the man slid down the roof, stopping at the rain gutter. Grabbing hold of the downspout, he used it as a ladder, then scuttled to the sidewalk and vanished into a nearby alley.

"I don't believe it!" Joe yelled, jumping forward. "That's Cass Carroll!"

Chapter

Ten

FRANK HARDY TOOK OFF across the street just behind his brother. Before they reached the far sidewalk, Officer Tiso came charging out the front door of Madame Strulenka's boarding-house.

"He went down the alley," Frank cried, leading the way.

Tiso explained what had happened as they ran. The brief words came out in time to their steps. "False wall in the attic—a dormitory—illegal aliens—only one there—our friend—"

"He went down this way," Frank said, pointing.

Tiso took the lead and peeled off into the dark passageway.

"Carroll won't get far," the officer said confidently. "We've got roving units patrolling the area. I'll alert—"

As Tiso reached for his walkie-talkie, a metal garbage can came flying out of the darkness ahead. It caught the officer across the chest and sent him bouncing against a wall before sinking to the ground.

Frank was at Tiso's side. "Are you all right?"

The officer pushed him away. "Go! Try to make sure he doesn't get away!" He glared at Frank. "I'll call for help. Go!"

Joe had already run ahead. "I see him!" he yelled, pointing. "On top of that shed."

The ramshackle shed leaned against the back wall of a brick building. Its rough wood planks were gray with age, and Frank wouldn't have thought they could support a person's weight.

But Joe was scrambling up the side as Cass Carroll ran across the shanty's tar-paper roof.

"We've got him!" Joe called back. "There's a fence."

As Frank reached his brother, he saw their quarry take a leap from the roof and grab on to the top of the ten-foot-high board fence that cut off the alleyway.

The guy heaved himself up, clamping an arm over the top of the fence. He swung himself onto the thin edge of the boards and, astonishingly, walked the top of the fence as if it were a tightrope.

"What is he, part cat?" Frank muttered.

Joe had already jumped for the fence. Carroll

was now halfway down the alley, on the far side, clambering onto the fire escape of an old tenement building.

"Go over and drop to the ground!" Frank shouted to his brother. "We'll never be able to pull the trick he did!"

Joe scrambled over the fence and landed hard on the broken cement below. A second later Frank followed. They ran to where the fire escape loomed overhead. Frank twined his fingers together to make a cup out of his hands and hunched down. Joe didn't need any more directions. He put the toe of his right shoe into the stirrup that Frank had constructed. As Joe jumped, Frank began to straighten his thighs and back and, catching his brother's upward momentum, heaved him skyward.

Catching the bottom of the fire-escape ladder, Joe climbed like a squirrel. He reached the first landing, then released the ladder for Frank and went pounding up the cast-iron stairs.

The bottom of the metal ladder landed with a shattering noise that resounded through the alley. Frank tore his way up the rungs, then jumped for the iron stairs that led to the roof. Joe was a floor ahead of him. Carroll was two floors ahead of Joe.

With every pounding footstep, the metal framework shook.

Frank couldn't help thinking that the thing was ancient. Just how long would those rusty bolts hold?

In fact, flakes of rust were fluttering down on him like reddish brown snow. Then came a metallic shriek from high above.

Frank peered up through the metal latticework. Carroll had tried to pull himself onto the roof, and one of the metal handholds had broken off.

He turned and threw the rusty iron rod down on his pursuers.

Joe dodged as the missile hit a crossbar over his head with a vicious clang and spun out into the air. He didn't pause but forged his way upward. The bar clattered on the cement alleyway below.

Nice guy, Frank thought. I wonder what Bess ever saw in him.

He charged up the next flight of stairs as first Carroll, then Joe, disappeared over the edge of the building onto the roof.

Even though Frank was alone on the fire escape now, it seemed more wobbly than ever. It sounded as if it were trying to rattle itself to pieces.

At last he reached the top. Vaulting over the low wall that ran around the roof's perimeter, Frank landed running.

All around him, Little Panaslava spread out like a patchwork quilt, the roofs of the buildings in different colors and heights. Old houses had sloping roofs of pinkish tiles or blue slate, patched in places with modern gray asphalt replacements. Tenement buildings featured roofs of gray gravel or faded black tar paper.

Carroll had reached the roof of an adjacent tenement and wasn't slowing down. He definitely has the home advantage, Frank thought. The fugitive reached the end of the second roof, with Joe still close behind. The next building was a story lower.

Without missing a beat, Carroll jumped.

A second or two later, Joe took off, too, and made a safe landing. And just a moment after that, Frank hurtled through the air.

Frank knew, because of his takeoff, that he was going to land badly on the gravel roof, but he remembered his karate. Part of that art was knowing how to fall. When Frank hit the roof, he rolled, which spread out the impact. He'd lost a second because of the fall but sprang back to his feet unhurt. Dodging around chimneys and TV antennas, Frank raced after Joe and Carroll.

The next building rose up two stories higher. Cass ran straight for a window level with the roof he was on. It was as if he was ready to smash through the pane of glass to enter the building. Then, without warning, a woman appeared in the window and opened it, screaming at the sight of Cass Carroll flying straight at her.

Instead of jumping through the opening, Carroll landed and scrambled up the window frame as if he were part monkey. From the top of that window, he leaped for the ledge of the next, then made his way up to the roof gutter.

Joe also leaped across the short distance and landed on the window ledge, coming face-to-face with the screaming woman. He stood for a moment, crouched with his hands on his knees, breathing hard.

Without missing a step, Frank leaped onto his brother's back and used him as a human ladder to reach the top of the window frame. He thrust himself upward, grabbed the bottom of the window frame above, and pulled himself up. Digging the toe of his shoe into the mortar between bricks for some sort of foothold, he worked his way upward. At the top of the second window, Frank grabbed for the gutter.

Frank got a one-handed hold and hauled himself up eye-level with the roof. One moment Carroll was nowhere to be seen, and the next he was in Frank's face, swinging a plank in both hands like a giant flyswatter.

Frank instinctively let go of his hold and pushed off with his feet as he dropped. The board slashed through the air where his head had been a second earlier, and splintered and snapped as it made contact with the edge of the roof.

Frank tried to go limp as he fell back to the lower roof. He needed to absorb as much of the shock of landing as possible. But in a split second, he realized that Joe had leaped back to this roof and was directly beneath him. Frank twisted his body to one side and just missed his brother. Pain lanced through his ankles and lower legs when he hit. He dropped heavily onto his side, then sat up.

"You okay, Frank?" Joe asked, giving his brother a helping hand.

"Nothing broken," Frank replied, testing his weight on his feet.

"Then come over here and help!"

Joe ran a few paces toward the back of the building where a ladder was stacked on some old wood. It was a crude thing, knocked together from two-by-fours and scrap lumber. From the way Joe was struggling, Frank guessed it was pretty heavy.

Frank stumbled over to lend a hand. In a moment they had it up. It reached just under the roofline of the adjoining building.

"This time, you go first," Frank said, panting.

Joe climbed up, carefully raising his head the last few inches. "Yesss!" he cried down to Frank. "We have him this time."

Frank climbed up after Joe and felt his adrenaline rush calming.

Carroll had run out of running room. He stood on top of the last tenement on the block. Three of the building's four corners were topped by matching parapets. The fourth corner, to Frank's right, where Carroll stood, had no parapet, only a yawning gap over the alley below. The closest building across the alley was more than ten feet away—and one story down.

As Frank scanned the roof a second time, he did see a way out. The parapet across the length of building from where Cass stood had been cut away to allow access to a fire escape.

Carroll must have seen it at the same time Frank did, because he began running the length of the roof toward it.

"Cut him off!" Frank shouted to Joe.

Carroll couldn't hope to win this race. The Hardys' ladder was much closer to the fire escape. They were in position to block Carroll before he was halfway there.

Then the fugitive did something truly weird. He skidded to a stop, spun around, and sprinted back for the end of the roof he'd just left!

"Stop!" Frank yelled, pounding after him. "You'll kill yourself!"

Carroll didn't stop. Legs furiously pumping, he flew off the roof.

Frank lurched to a stop just inches before the roof ended. He stared in horror as Carroll sailed out over the alleyway, his legs still pumping. No way could he reach the opposite rooftop, or even its edge. Gravity was against him.

Frank couldn't turn away. He saw Carroll miss the roof by at least a yard and then gaped in shock as Cass caught hold of the fire escape that ran down the back of the building.

The crash of Cass's impact bounced off the fire escape and reverberated along the alley, but he held on, legs dangling. Without looking back, he swung his lower body onto the stairway and started his descent.

"Man!" Joe breathed heavily next to Frank. "That guy is very good."

"Or very desperate," Frank concluded.

Frank started running toward the front of the building. "You take the fire escape," he yelled at Joe. He stopped and turned, exactly as Cass had done. "I'm going after him."

Joe stared. "Are you crazy?"

"Just practical," Frank replied. "Someone has to stay right on his tail. But both of us don't need to risk our necks."

Joe opened his mouth to argue, but Frank had already started his sprint to the edge of the roof. Frank dashed past his brother and leaped as far as he could into the air.

Frank's legs kept running, as if he could gain traction on thin air. He flew out and down. He was below the roof line now, the far wall swinging toward him.

He smashed into the fire escape. Pain screamed through his chest and ribs, and he bounced backward. Frank clutched at the metal balcony with a strength born of desperation. If he messed this up, the next stop was six stories straight down.

Frank's clawing fingers caught hold, and he swung himself up and over onto the balcony. Carroll was halfway down, but he had halted to watch Frank. Frank forced himself down the steep, rusty stairway. He'd probably still wind up breaking his neck, he thought.

Frank didn't pause to check on how Carroll was doing. All he had to do was keep the pressure on, stay on Carroll's back.

Suddenly, there were no more stairs, only a ladder. Carroll was down on the ground, running for the mouth of the alley. Frank leaped for a second time, landing on top of a Dumpster, then jumped to the ground. He struggled to keep the fear of losing sight of Cass out of his head, and lost. How could Carroll run like that? If he got out of sight, even for a second . . .

A streak of blue shot into the alleyway and screeched to a halt. Carroll's escape route was blocked by a police car—no. Frank did a double take. It was Nancy's car.

Carroll almost crashed head-on into the sudden roadblock. Instead, he skidded to a halt, ran to the side, and yanked the driver's door open. There was a brief struggle before Nancy was hauled out of the car and tumbled to the pavement. Carroll flung himself inside.

Faster, Frank, he told himself. Get to Nancy. Did she hold on to the car keys?

The blue car's engine roared to life just as Frank reached its hood. Nancy had already scrambled out of the way. It was all up to Frank. . . .

He pounced on the door, but even as he grabbed the handle, the car leaped into motion, screaming in reverse. Frank was thrown to the ground.

He pushed himself up on hands and knees. Nancy's car was now a few dozen yards away, screeching to a stop. Then, wheels squealing, it was moving forward again.

Straight at him.

Chapter

Eleven

JOE HARDY rounded the corner of the building to find a nightmare in progress. Frank lay sprawled at the mouth of the alley, with a car powering up to run over him.

Yelling, Joe dashed forward, but there was no way he could beat the car to its target.

The sound of tortured rubber filled the air as the wheels spun against the brake. Then the driver threw the car into motion.

The vehicle made a leap forward, but then the engine simply quit. Instead of gaining speed, the car slowed down, as if the brakes had been applied. Frank had plenty of time to get out of the way of the car as it coasted down the alleyway to a stop.

Joe charged up to the driver's door and threw it open. "Get out!" he yelled. Sure enough, the driver—tall, slim, with a mop of long black hair—was the fugitive they'd been chasing. Without a second thought, Joe brought a fist up from knee level to the guy's jaw. Carroll managed to glare at Joe in defeat before he toppled to the ground, unconscious.

Shaking his stinging knuckles, Joe glanced over at Frank, who had gotten to his feet. They exchanged a shaky grin.

"You're a lucky guy. If whoever owns this car had paid for a tune-up, you'd be smeared all over this street."

"You can thank me for that," a girl said, stepping over to Frank.

"Nancy!" Joe sputtered.

"It's my car," she said, smiling but pale-faced. "And I had a tune-up last week, thank you. But before I was so rudely ejected from my car, I flicked on the kill switch of my antitheft system. It's supposed to let the engine run for a little bit, then cut it out."

"Your sense of timing is impeccable," Frank said. He threw an arm around Nancy's shoulders, wincing from the pain of his complaining muscles.

"I'm even more impressed by your sense of geography," Joe said. "How did you know Carroll would turn up here?"

"I didn't," Nancy confessed. "But I figured if I got my car and cruised around the far side of the block, I stood a good chance of getting ahead of the chase." She gestured toward the inert figure.

"I'd hoped to speak with Cass alone, for a minute or two, but—"

Nancy was interrupted by a groan from the pavement.

"Well, well, Carroll," Joe cut in, hauling the guy to his feet. "The next tune you'll be singing is 'Jailhouse Rock.'"

"I hate to tell you guys," Nancy said with some annoyance, her hands on her hips, "but this is not Cass Carroll."

"What?" Joe swung the limp figure around to get a good look at him. "He matches the description: tall, thin, long black hair—"

Joe sighed and gave up. Now that the man was up close, Joe could see that his features didn't match Carroll's at all. This guy's cheekbones were too high, and his nose was more beaky. But if he wasn't Cass . . .

"So why was he running like a lunatic?" Joe demanded.

"Officer Tiso said he'd been flushed out of his hiding place. He's an illegal," Frank said, suddenly feeling sorry for their captive. "My guess is he didn't want to be shipped back to Panaslava."

"Oh, yeah," a snide voice jeered from behind Joe. "It's a terrible thing for filthy Panaslavans to come pushing their way into the good old U.S. of A. Why doesn't he just go back where he belongs."

Still holding on to the half-conscious man who was not Cass, Joe turned around. Behind them, a crowd had gathered, and front and center stood Tad Vlachovic—with his mouth going.

"These Americans were always happy to have Panaslavans come to River Heights when they could put them to work in their factories for pennies," Tad shouted.

A murmur of agreement ran through the crowd.

"And when we were fighting Communists, America could feel patriotic helping us refugees. All we had to do was take the filthiest jobs for the lowest pay and keep quiet."

The murmur turned into a growl.

"My dad worked himself to death for them. Now they have no more jobs for us, and so they hunt us down like him." Tad pointed to the man in Joe's arms. "This is the real America!"

"Vlachovic, get off it," Joe growled. "Did I know this guy was here illegally? No. What I do know is that he injured a cop who is investigating a murder in *your* community. He almost did me in with a metal bar, nearly brained my brother with a two-by-four, and then tried to run him over—after physically throwing this woman from her car!"

The unfriendly looks in the crowd began to shift from Joe, Frank, and Nancy toward Tad and the illegal alien.

Tad's face went red. He changed his attack to try to win back the crowd's sympathy. "So, you're going to be big shots and turn him over to the cops. Why don't you let him go?"

"Hey," Frank spoke up. "We're trying to solve a murder in Little Panaslava. Would you rather we just stay out of it?"

A voice came from the rear of the crowd. "No! We need to stop crime in our streets!" The people around the unidentified man murmured their agreement as Tad turned around, looking for the speaker.

"Why don't you give it up, Tad?" Nancy cut in angrily. "You talk a good game about what a raw deal you got while your neighbors are out *earning* the things you're so jealous of."

"She right." A heavily accented voice came from the crowd. "I work for a living. All he does is steal."

His face a mask of fury, Tad whipped around, his hand going into the pocket of his leather jacket. Then the sound of approaching sirens filled the air, and Tad, like a number of people on the street, abruptly vanished.

Police cruisers blocked either end of the alley, and armed officers converged on them. "All of you keep your hands where we can see them!" a gruff voice commanded.

Joe released the false Cass Carroll and raised his hands.

The illegal alien staggered forward, then finally saw the police. He silently brought his hands into the air.

Another wave of police cruisers arrived as the officers began questioning the participants in the recent drama. Chief McGinnis joined Nancy, Frank, and Joe.

"The patrols have been looking for you since Officer Tiso called in. Where were you?"

Joe and Frank smiled weakly. "Don't ask," they said in unison.

"How is Officer Tiso?" Nancy asked.

"He's been picked up by an ambulance and should be all right," the chief informed them. "Then, when we got reports of a scuffle on this block, we figured it must be you." Chief McGinnis turned to the downcast fugitive, who stood with his head bowed as an officer handcuffed his wrists behind him.

"We've got a lot of questions to ask you, Mr. Carroll," McGinnis began. Then his eyes narrowed as the prisoner raised his face.

"Wait just a minute," the chief said. "This isn't Cass Carroll, or Casimir Karolyi, or whatever name he's going by today."

The chief stared at the captive. "I don't know who this guy is, but he's not the man we're looking for." The chief turned to the young detectives for an explanation.

"He probably ran because he's here illegally," Frank said slowly. "I guess he panicked."

"Panic or not, he assaulted a police officer—and created a public disturbance," McGinnis said. "We're taking him in, and I'd like the three of you to come in and give statements."

They arrived in the detectives' section of police headquarters to find Madame Strulenka sitting in front of one of the desks. To Joe, the elegant lady seemed suddenly older, her face harder.

Madame Strulenka glared at Nancy and the Hardys. "What are you doing here?" she demanded.

"We had an interesting time with one of your tenants," Joe said. "A brisk chase across the rooftops, and whenever things got boring, he tried to kill us."

"I have nothing to say," she snapped. "I'm waiting for my lawyer."

"Why did you do it?" Nancy asked. "Why board illegal aliens?"

"To you they are this thing—illegal aliens. What do you know? They are my people, my responsibility." Madame Strulenka straightened her shoulders. "My family was one of the greatest in Sarabia—in all Panaslava. We had houses, land, servants. There, I wouldn't have even spoken to an upstart like Egon Marek—some little mountain *grof* from Zelenogora. But Sarabians? We are family."

"Grofina—that means countess," Nancy said. "And Egon is a *grof?* A count?"

"His family claimed the title, under his mousy little king—his precious Karol Boris."

"Karol," Nancy repeated. "That's Panaslavan for king?"

Madame Strulenka rolled her eyes and nodded

as if it were painful to have to educate such idiots.

Joe, however, was watching the changing expression on Nancy's face. "What's up, Drew?"

"I wonder," she said. "Cass's last name is Carroll, and he has a passport in a different but similar name. Casimir *Karolyi*."

She leaned excitedly toward Joe. "Do you see where I'm going?"

He shook his head. "Not at all. How about you, Frank?"

His brother looked equally baffled.

"Cass Carroll—Casimir Karolyi? Cass Americanized his name from Casimir Karolyi," Nancy said.

"I don't get it," Joe replied.

Nancy's face was pink with excitement as she tried to explain. "We've all been scratching our heads, wondering why Pavel Raskol, who served the exiled King Boris Ladinovic, would have anything to do with Cass Carroll."

Frank and Joe nodded. So far, so good.

"But," Nancy said, "try this question instead: Why would someone who served *Karol Boris* get in touch with a Casimir *Karolyi* right after the king was killed?"

The light began to dawn in Joe's head. "You mean?"

Nancy nodded. "Cass could be the heir to the Panaslavan throne."

Chapter

Twelve

THAT'S THE MOST ridiculous idea I ever heard!"
Chuck Bascomb scoffed. "I think it even beats
out young Mr. Hardy's brilliant deduction that
the late Mr. Raskol was actually the Haiduk in
disguise."

Nancy could feel her face burning. Acting on
her brainstorm, she, Frank, and Joe had headed
for Chief McGinnis's office to share her theory
with Bascomb, who was now taking potshots at
it.

Joe cheerfully joined in. "You've got to admit,
Nancy, it is kind of out there. After all, lots of
people in this country have the last name *King,*
and they aren't royalty. That creepy Tad's last
name is Vlachovic, but he's not related to any
Panaslavan kings."

"I thought you'd have liked my idea, Joe,"

Nancy replied sweetly. "It ties in with yours. Raskol is the Haiduk, and he was sent to River Heights to kill the royal heir."

"And what romance novel did you pick that idea out of?" Bascomb mocked. "Could we at least *try* to keep this conversation based in the real world?"

"Okay, maybe Raskol isn't the Haiduk, but we know Cass has more than one name," Nancy replied. "Does anyone have a better suggestion for why Cass was in Raskol's car?"

"He could have been hitchhiking," the State Department man said sourly.

Frank shook his head. "If I had a hitchhiker who was yelling at me the way Cass was yelling in that car, I don't think I'd have invited him back to my motel room." He frowned in thought. "Raskol's involvement with the assassinated Panaslavan king suggests there's a political motive in this case. If Cass turns out to have some connection to royalty, that would tie in on the political side."

He turned to Chief McGinnis. "At least it would be worth checking out."

"I'm not going to bother my contacts—" Bascomb began.

"Luckily, you won't have to, Mr. Bascomb," Chief McGinnis cut in. "The University of Chicago has a very good center of Eastern European studies. We'll make inquiries there."

He got up from behind his desk. "In the meantime, our house-to-house in Little Panaslava has turned up a gambling club in someone's cellar. But we haven't had a glimpse of Cass Carroll—or a hint that the Haiduk really is in town."

"He's a professional, Chief McGinnis," Bascomb reminded him. "We can't expect—"

"We're continuing the search," the chief said, cutting Bascomb off. "In the meantime, I have work to do—"

So don't let the door hit you on your way out, Nancy silently finished his sentence.

The Hardys followed Nancy as she arranged to get her car released from the impound lot, where the police had driven it.

"It's like I told you, Frank," Joe said to his brother as Nancy filled out forms. "If a girl even gets a whiff of royalty, she goes crazy. It's not enough that this guy Carroll is good-looking or foreign or a potential rock star. No, he's got to be a prince."

He grinned at Nancy. "You going to tell Bess about this? She'll just die if she finds out she's going out with a king's nephew, or grandson, or whatever. What do you think he is, the Grand Duke of Heavy Metal?"

"Grand Dude, maybe," Frank suggested.

Nancy wasn't laughing.

Bess! She hadn't thought of Bess since they'd set out to interview the band that morning. Guiltily, Nancy remembered how Bess had jumped out of her car at a stoplight because Nancy insisted on turning Cass's strongbox over to the police. Not only did Nancy feel an urgent need to make up with her friend, she knew that Bess should know how the case was going. She might even know who Cass was!

"Guys," Nancy said, turning to Frank and Joe. "I didn't tell you this before, but Bess flipped out when I said we had to bring in Cass's strongbox. She actually bailed out of my car at a stoplight."

Frank gave her a shrewd look. "That's why she didn't come in with you."

"Wow!" Joe exclaimed. "That doesn't sound like our bubbly Bess."

"She's really hung up on Cass," Nancy said miserably. "Anyway, I want to tell her what's happened now, but—"

"You're afraid she'll just slam the door in your face," Frank finished.

"But maybe if you had a couple of handsome young men along, a couple of her own friends, she might let them in—and you, too," Joe said with a smile.

Nancy tapped the side of Joe's head with a finger. "What a clever idea, Joe! Now, if you could only suggest where I could find those handsome guys . . ."

Joe gave her a dirty look, but Frank laughed. "I don't know if you have time to waste. Maybe you should just work with the raw materials you've got here."

"Thanks, Frank," Nancy said. "Do you need a ride?"

"No, you'd just have to drive us back down

here to get our car," Frank said. "You lead the way, and we'll follow."

It was almost suppertime when Nancy arrived at the Marvin house, with Frank and Joe right behind her.

As she pulled up, she spotted a figure standing in the drive, and her heart sank. It was Brenda Carlton, wearing an open trench coat over a red silk minidress. Nancy decided it was probably her idea of what a stylish girl reporter would wear on a stakeout.

Brenda's father owned *Today's Times,* the sleazier of the two newspapers in River Heights. That was the only reason her byline appeared in the paper at all. She was *not* a good reporter. In fact, she was lazy, gossipy, and biased, and she'd do anything she could to get at her biggest investigative rival: Nancy Drew.

"Nancy!" Brenda called.

Nancy sighed. It was too late to hit the gas and pass by. She parked the car and got out.

"Oh! Frank and Joe Hardy!" Brenda crowed triumphantly as the boys pulled up as well. Brenda smelled a story. There would be no getting rid of her now.

"What brings you out here, Brenda?" Nancy asked unhappily.

"I'm freezing!" Brenda complained. "And it's just because Mr. and Mrs. Marvin are being silly about my interviewing Bess."

"Why would you want to interview Bess?" Nancy asked, her heart sinking further.

"Bess has been going out with Cass Carroll, the main suspect in the Raskol murder case," Brenda said, trailing after Nancy and the boys as they headed for the door. "But am I telling you anything new? Anyway, I want to do a story. I thought I could call it 'Dating a Dangerous Man.'"

Nancy felt her lips compress in a tight line. This would be a typical Brenda Carlton story—a grain of truth mixed with a ton of sleaze.

She pressed the doorbell. "Wasn't that the title of a TV movie?"

"Well, I could change it," Brenda said bigheartedly, trying to get beside Nancy at the door. "Maybe if you talked to the Marvins for me—"

Nancy sent a pleading look to the Hardys as the door opened. The brothers slipped into formation, easily blocking Brenda as Nancy stepped into the house.

"At least you could ask them," Nancy heard Brenda call as the door shut.

"Sorry about that, Mrs. Marvin," Nancy said to Bess's mother.

"I'm the one who should be sorry." Mrs. Marvin peered out the window in annoyance. "That crazy girl has been out there almost an hour now. She came up and told us it would be best if Bess got her side of the story out in public before her boyfriend was arrested."

She sighed. "We had a bit of a talk about this Cass Carroll—Bess, her father, and I. Then, when Brenda wouldn't leave, Bess's dad suggested Bess get out of here. That way, the cat would be watching an empty mousehole. He and Bess went out the kitchen door and cut across the backyard to our neighbors' house. They borrowed a car and went to the Faynes'."

Mrs. Marvin smiled as Nancy burst into laughter. "Good for them," Nancy cheered.

"But I've been stuck here, under siege." Bess's mom peered out the window again. "Now she's got reinforcements—two young men. Wait a minute, I recognize them. They're your friends from Bayport, the Hardys."

"Frank and Joe ran a little interference for me," Nancy admitted. "They'll keep Brenda outside."

"I saw her before on a mobile phone, so I suspect she was calling for help." Mrs. Marvin shook her head. "This will only get worse before it gets better."

Through the front window, Nancy saw a van pull up and park in front of her car. "I think you're right," she said. A young man with a camera got out.

"Help me close these drapes," Mrs. Marvin said as the man aimed his camera at the front windows.

They managed to shut off his view of inside the house, but the photographer still shot half a roll, Nancy estimated, judging from the flashes of light outside.

"These news people certainly have nerve," Bess's mother complained. "I'm going to step out there and give him a piece of my mind." She marched to the front door.

Taking a deep breath, Mrs. Marvin threw open the door and advanced on the surprised photographer. "What do you think you're doing here, young man?" she demanded in a loud voice. "This is private property, you know. You're trespassing. I'd be within my rights to shoot you—wouldn't I, Howard?" she shouted toward the window where Nancy stood.

Nancy twitched the curtains open to watch the show, but she didn't get to enjoy much of it because the phone started to ring. She went to the kitchen extension and picked it up.

"Hello," Nancy said. But she barely got that much out before a tight voice let loose a rush of words.

"Bess, is that you? I'm sorry, so very sorry—"

Nancy was too surprised to speak. She immediately recognized the British accent on the other end of the line. It was Cass Carroll.

Chapter

Thirteen

I KNOW EVERYTHING seems to point at me being a murderer, Bess," Cass Carroll said hurriedly. "But you've got to believe I didn't kill poor Raskol. Bess, say something. Say that you believe me."

"Cass," Nancy said, finally getting her breath back. "Bess isn't here. This is Nancy—Nancy Drew."

"What?" Cass sounded vaguely lost. Nancy realized he must have been concentrating solely on getting his message across to Bess. And now she'd derailed his train of thought.

"It's Nancy," she repeated. "We met at the club last night."

Had it really been only last night that all this had started?

"Of course," Cass said, trying to sound polite. "Ah—do you expect Bess back soon?"

"I'm not sure," Nancy replied honestly. "She's staying at her cousin George's because of a little media trouble. There are people here who want to interview her about you."

Nancy heard an unhappy intake of breath on the other end of the line.

Now is the time to push, she thought. Either I'm right, or he'll tell me I'm crazy.

"I suppose you've dealt with that all your life," Nancy said. "The media, I mean. I wondered why you took the news of King Boris's death so hard, but now I understand."

"My father was never a king," Cass said bitterly. "Except in his own private dream world. 'Casimir,' he used to say, 'we are Ladinovics, the true heirs of Panaslava, the royal family, our country's last resort.'

"The poor—" The rumble of a truck drowned out Cass's words. Nancy realized he must be calling from an outdoor pay phone. "He'd tell me all about my duty to Panaslava—in French! We lived in Paris, I spoke French better than any of the Panaslavan dialects he and Mother tried to teach me. I had a tutor for English, because Father thought that was the international language of diplomacy. He didn't speak the language well, and he felt that put him at a disadvantage."

The bitterness increased in Cass's voice. "My

grandfather, Old Boris, left Panaslava, but my father was determined to go back, to regain the throne—"

Cass's voice broke. "And in the end, his stupid schemes got him killed."

"Cass, whatever happened between you and Pavel Raskol, you've got to clear it up." Nancy was holding the telephone receiver so hard, her hand hurt. "Right now you're the prime suspect in the man's murder. I don't think you did it— and neither does Bess," she added quickly. "But there's a manhunt on for you. The longer you stay in hiding, the more guilty you look.

"Listen to me," Nancy pleaded. "I know what I'm talking about. It will be much better if you come in—"

"I can't do that," Cass replied. Then, sounding more like a prince, he said, "I *won't* do that. I am now the target myself."

Nancy heard a sudden, familiar noise in the background—sirens. *"Zut! Les flics!"* Cass cried in French. Then the phone went dead.

After hanging up, Nancy stared at the phone in the Marvins' kitchen, wishing she could have found the words to persuade Cass to end the manhunt for him. Then again, she thought, perhaps it was now over. Nancy understood enough French to know that *les flics* meant the police. The siren she had heard was a police siren.

Her thoughts were interrupted by Mrs. Marvin slamming the front door.

"Success," Bess's mother reported with some satisfaction. "He didn't take a single picture."

"I'm glad," Nancy said distractedly, though *shaken* would have described better how she felt. She had proven her theory, but there was more to it than she had guessed. Cass had said he was now a target.

"I have to go, Mrs. Marvin," Nancy said. "If you speak to Bess, tell her I'll catch up with her at George's."

"I certainly will, dear," Mrs. Marvin replied, glancing out at Brenda. "And good luck out there."

Nancy barreled out the front door and made it to the sidewalk before Brenda pounced on her. "Will they let Bess speak with me?"

"They have no comment," Nancy said, which she figured was true enough. "And neither does Bess." That, however, probably wasn't true. Nancy figured her friend would have a lot to say when she finally saw her.

Frank and Joe appeared, having left the safety of their car.

"That's not good enough, Drew!" An ugly expression passed over Brenda's pretty but sharp-featured face. "I promised Dad—I mean, I'm determined to get a good story here. If this doesn't pan out, that means I've got to get a story from *you.*"

She examined Nancy and the Hardys. "Are you three involved in the Carroll investigation?"

"I wouldn't say directly," Frank answered, carefully shading the truth.

"I have reports that you chased him across Little Panaslava this afternoon," Brenda countered.

Nancy sighed. Brenda did sometimes listen to the police radio monitor in the newsroom at *Today's Times*. It was just too bad that she'd had to do it this afternoon.

"And lost him," Brenda charged. Nancy was gratified to hear that she didn't listen very closely.

"You were mentioned in those reports, too," Brenda went on, focusing on Nancy.

"You know how news can get exaggerated," Nancy answered.

"The plain facts are a lot more boring," Frank said, downplaying the whole incident.

"Oh." Brenda's wicked grin shriveled, and she switched targets again. "Is it true that the feds sent you guys here to find an international assassin?"

The boys glanced at Nancy in astonishment. Nancy shrugged. Surely, that hadn't been on the police radio.

"Sure," Joe replied sarcastically. "We were brought here on a secret government UFO, piloted by Elvis."

All through Brenda's inquisition, Nancy, Frank, and Joe had been retreating to their cars. At this point, Frank opened their car door.

"Don't think you can avoid the eye of the press

by running away," Brenda warned. "I have a car, too."

Her bright red buzz-bomb was the exact same shade as her minidress and lipstick.

"Yeah," Frank said dryly. "We noticed."

"You lead," Nancy whispered to the boys. "I'll follow."

But Brenda's eavesdropping abilities were as good as ever. "So will I," she threatened.

Joe rolled his eyes in disgust. "Let's just get out of here."

Frank tossed his brother the keys to their rental car. "I'll ride with Nancy."

Joe pulled away from the curb, followed by Nancy and Frank and, a second later, Brenda.

"Does he know where he's going?" Nancy asked as she leaned into a sharp right turn, following Joe.

"I don't think so," Frank replied.

Joe continued to lead them on a zigzag course through the neighborhood.

"I think he's lost," Nancy said.

"Probably, but let's not stop the car to find out," Frank said. Then he smiled. "Maybe Ms. Carlton will run out of gas."

"That would be a first," Nancy said, laughing.

At last, though, Nancy began to see a method in Joe's seeming madness. He was looking for the route they had taken coming from the police station, one of the few routes he knew in River Heights. She wasn't exactly thrilled.

Nancy had yet to tell Frank and Joe about

Cass's phone call, let alone Bess. If they showed up at the station, she knew she'd feel obligated to report it to Chief McGinnis.

He wouldn't much care about Cass's admission that he was, in fact, Prince Casimir Ladinovic. But they'd be very interested in the fact that he'd tried to contact Bess Marvin. They'd try to use her as bait to bring him in.

Nancy shook her head. She'd hurt Bess enough already. She couldn't set her up for that.

Nancy was right. Five minutes later Joe finally parked across the street from police headquarters. Nancy found a spot nearby.

Brenda pulled up right in front of the building, parking in a handicapped space.

Brenda stood on the steps to the station house and yelled at the Hardys and Nancy across the street. "See, you couldn't lose me!" she boasted. "I know this town like the back of my hand."

Nancy and Frank quickly joined Joe, who was standing by his car watching Brenda as if she were part of a freak show.

"Okay, Joe," Frank whispered to his brother. "What do we do with her now?"

Joe's eyes danced with mischief. "I just thought that the lovely reporter would enjoy the chance to interview the equally charming State Department agent."

"You really like Bascomb, don't you?" Frank asked jokingly, then added, "I only hope he's still in."

As Joe passed Brenda, she just about attached

herself to him. He took her past the desk sergeant, down the hall, and into the detectives' room. Chuck Bascomb still sat at his borrowed desk.

"Mr. Bascomb of the State Department, meet Brenda Carlton of *Today's Times,* a local newspaper."

Brenda's eyes had gone big, and her nose was almost twitching with excitement.

"Ms. Carlton has been asking us all sorts of questions," Joe went on. "I thought you'd prefer to deal with the rumors she's heard directly."

If looks could kill, Bascomb's would have left Joe shriveled and smoking on the floor.

Nancy smothered a laugh as she and the boys retreated. "He's never going to forgive you for this," she whispered to Joe.

Before they could escape, however, Chief McGinnis appeared. "Nancy, are you still here?" he said in surprise. Then he noticed Brenda and quickly retreated, beckoning the young people to follow.

"I just got off the phone with a Professor Smiley at the university," the chief said when he had slipped into an office and closed the door. "He knows about these royal things, and he says there *is* a Casimir Ladinovic. And with the death of Boris, he's the heir to the throne of Panaslava."

Nancy didn't know whether to look surprised or guilty. She already had proof that Cass was Prince Casimir—from his own mouth. But she couldn't tell the chief how Cass felt about the throne of Panaslava, not without giving away the phone call she'd had with him at Bess's house.

Chief McGinnis went on, however. "But this prince will have a problem getting crowned. After King Boris was assassinated, the royal regalia disappeared from Paris."

He shrugged. "Not that it sounds as though Panaslava had a lot in the crown jewels department. When they were smuggled out of the country after the war, they fit into a single briefcase."

Chapter

Fourteen

FRANK AND JOE HARDY stared open-mouthed at Nancy and the chief.

"Next, I checked with Interpol to see whether our Casimir Karolyi, alias Cass Carroll, was, in fact, Casimir Ladinovic, King Boris's son," Chief McGinnis continued. "And guess what?"

The chief looked as if he were ready to drop a bombshell, which was the way it hit the Hardys. "About six months ago, young Casimir Ladinovic left Paris. He was given a special passport so he wouldn't be recognized as a prince—they call it traveling incognito. That passport was made out to Casimir Karolyi."

Joe smacked himself in the forehead. "Incognito! That's the name of Cass Carroll's band! It was sitting in front of us all this time!" He turned to Nancy. "Well, you certainly called this one right—way ahead of the rest of us."

Nancy only shook her head. "I guess the band name was his little joke."

"Or," Frank suggested, "just a cool name for a band."

"Thanks for the information, Chief," Nancy said calmly.

Joe was surprised. Nancy didn't sound half as triumphant as he would have after having been proven right.

Nancy glanced quickly at the office door. "Now the question is, can we get out of here without Brenda Carlton latching onto us again?"

Luckily, Brenda was still too busy badgering Chuck Bascomb to notice the Hardys and Nancy escaping.

As they headed down the stationhouse steps, Nancy said, "I have got to talk to Bess." Joe thought she sounded exhausted.

"I don't know how to put this so you won't misunderstand me," Joe began. His words certainly caught Frank and Nancy's attention.

"What is it, Joe?" Frank asked, his voice full of concern.

"I need something to eat," Joe replied. "It's past our supper time. Got you going, didn't I?" He laughed and slapped his brother on the back.

Nancy smiled weakly but said she really had to see Bess. "She was so angry at me when she got out of my car that I have to clear the air. Plus, it's been a very long day, and I have a lot to tell her."

"No," Joe responded, taking unaccustomed authority over Nancy. "You're exhausted, Nancy. You need some downtime—and food—before you face Bess."

"You may be right," Nancy concluded. "But—"

"But nothing," Frank interruped her. "Joe is right. We eat first, then you see Bess."

This time Nancy's smile was full of life. "It sure is nice to have two brothers ordering me around. Okay, where to?"

"Where else?" Joe said. "Old Egon's."

Egon laughed as the teenagers walked back into his café. "I hoped you'd be back," the host said with a smile. "But I didn't expect you so soon."

"Hi, Dedya Egon." Nancy paused for a second. "Or should I call you Grof Egon or Count?"

"Dedya will be fine," the old aristocrat replied quizzically. "Dedya—grandfather—outranks count, anyway. So, welcome again to my castle."

He led them to a private dining room beyond the public area and gave them menus. "Now I treat you to some Panaslavan specialties."

"Hey," Joe said, "you've got rabbit stew."

"Oh, yum," Nancy said dubiously. "You'd eat a rabbit?"

"I see there's also a venison goulash with kasha," Joe said. "If I order that, are you going to blame me for Bambi's mother?"

Nancy shook her head, smiling. "Not as long as I don't have to eat it."

Frank raised his eyebrows as he reviewed the menu. "Wiener schnitzel?" he said. "Is that a Panaslavan dish?"

"It's Austrian, really. But if your country is east of France and west of China, people expect to see Wiener schnitzel on the menu." Egon shrugged. "We make a perfectly good schnitzel, but it's not truly a native dish."

"Well, that rules out the schnitzel," Frank said, grinning. "When in Panaslava, eat as the Panaslavans do."

In the end Joe chose the venison, Nancy had a spicy chicken concoction called *paprikash,* and Frank tried the rabbit stew.

Old Egon approved of their selections.

"Dedya Egon," Nancy said. "This food is wonderful. I never knew chicken could be so rich."

Egon sat with them, taking tiny sips of a clear liquid from a glass scarcely larger than a thimble.

"Tell us some more about old Panaslava and King Boris, Dedya Egon, please?" Nancy cajoled.

"I promise I won't yawn," Joe added.

"Do you remember what I told you this afternoon?" the old man asked, but he didn't wait for an answer. "When the Vlachovics tried to rule us, our king still had many supporters. Old Boris lived in hiding among us like a bandit, a guerrilla. We would call him a *haiduk.*"

Joe gave Egon a sharp glance at the unexpected name. But the old man was lost in memories.

"I met Old Boris once." Egon's usual ironic smile was gone as he remembered. "I was a child when I was smuggled out of the country to Paris. There were many Panaslavan exiles there, many intrigues.

"Later, as a young man, I carried a gun. And I was ready to use it. We raised money to take an army back to Panaslava, to raise the flag of revolt against the Communists. Old Boris heard of our plan and talked sense to us young men. He had the Ladinovic look—handsome. His hair had gone gray, but he was still as tall and fit as I was back then."

"What did he say?" Nancy asked.

"He spoke of his life in the mountains, among people who loved him." Egon's features became stern. "'And I never won,' he said. 'How do you hope to win your fight when the people have already forgotten you?'"

"He stopped you from going back?" Joe shook his head. "I would have thought he'd have wanted to get the regime that threw him out. Why did he protect them?"

"Boris wasn't protecting them," Egon said. "He was protecting *us*. As I look back, I realize now we wouldn't have had a chance. We'd have gotten ourselves killed, along with a lot of innocent Panaslavans. And," he said as he put his little glass down on the table, "instead of being merely forgotten, people would remember the royal cause with hatred. Even though the Communists ruled Panaslava, Boris was protecting his people—and his crown—for another day."

"It sounds as if Boris would have made a great king," Nancy said quietly.

"I think so," Egon replied. "But then I'm prejudiced—he saved my life."

Excusing himself, Egon rose to visit at other tables.

"Well," Frank said after the café owner had left, "what did we learn from that?"

"It seems to me," Joe ventured, "that there isn't a lot of support for the Ladinovics taking over Panaslava again."

"No," Nancy said. "After what Dedya Egon said this afternoon about not much money being raised—and little of it actually reaching any of the factions—I don't think Bascomb's money theory holds up. Why would Raskol be collecting contributions for a war that the Ladinovics wanted to stay out of?"

"If he was hanging out with the royal family," Joe said, "Raskol had to know Cass, and Cass had to know him. That's why they were in the car together the other night. But what was Raskol saying that Cass didn't like?"

"Wait a second," Frank spoke up. "Do we know when Raskol left Paris? And more important, exactly when was Boris assassinated?"

"I haven't seen any reports about it in the papers or on television," Nancy said. She beckoned to Egon, who returned to their table. "That radio report you heard about the king's death—were there any more details?"

Egon shook his head. "But I received something the next day." He stepped into the coffee room and returned with a copy of the *International Herald Tribune*. "It's the best English-language newspaper in Paris. They printed a fairly long story. Feel free to read while I execute my duties as host."

"'Exiled Monarch Assassinated,'" Nancy read aloud when Egon had left them alone again. She sped silently through the story and then said, "According to this, Boris was shot on Friday, the day before we heard the news of his death. At first the news of the shooting was kept secret because he lingered for a while in a coma. Only when he died was an announcement made."

"That means Raskol must have been in Paris when the king was shot." Joe frowned in thought. "Is it possible that Raskol killed the king? And then headed here to take out the king's heir?"

"What would be his motive?" Frank asked.

Joe was stumped for a second, then thumped the table. "The crown jewels! Raskol wasn't getting any younger. Suppose he tried to leave the king's entourage and took the jewels for his retirement. Boris got in the way, and . . . bang. He comes to America to shut the prince's mouth about the missing jewels, but Cass got him first."

"There are enough holes in that story to drive a truck through," Frank said. "If Cass acted in self-defense, why would he be hiding from the police?"

"I wish I had an answer to that question," Nancy said.

"Still, the timing of Raskol's arrival means he had to have left Paris after Boris was shot," Frank said. "Maybe he came to River Heights to find Cass and tell him to come home."

Joe nodded. "There's the fact that Cass is the heir to the throne. Maybe the family wants him back home in Paris so they can crown him or something."

"But maybe he didn't want to go," Frank suggested. "By the time Raskol got to Cass, the king had already died. Cass has his own life over here now. A girlfriend"—he looked at Nancy, who shrugged—"and a possible record contract. Cass was on the verge of the American Dream, and here comes Raskol trying to drag him back to a title that has meant nothing for fifty years."

"I don't think he'd have gone back," Nancy said. She paused, a little flustered, then regained her train of thought. "You didn't see him when he heard about his father. The bitter way he called Boris the pretender to the throne."

Joe thought Nancy was about to continue explaining but was surprised when instead she turned to Frank and changed the subject. "It sounds as if you're accusing Cass of killing Raskol. But he wouldn't *have* to kill the guy—all he had to do was say no."

"Maybe Raskol wouldn't take no for an answer," Frank said, meeting her objection. "Maybe he threatened to tell the whole story and make Cass look bad. Brenda Carlton could have a field day with it. Imagine the headlines: 'Kid Turns Back on Dying Father to Become a Rock Star.'"

"There's no such thing as bad publicity for rock stars," Joe said. "The news that Cass is a prince would have sold a bazillion compact discs."

Frank raised a finger. "A record company public relations person might think that way, but would Cass? Raskol might have threatened his good name, his honor. That might be a very Panaslavan reason to kill someone."

"Cass doesn't come from Panaslava." Nancy put down her knife and fork and leaned across the table. "He comes from France. And he left there to get *away* from the whole Panaslavan royalty business."

Her voice was sharp as she raised her objections. Joe began to suspect she was keeping information from them. She seemed preoccupied.

"Whatever Cass did or didn't do, I'll bet one thing," Joe said, watching for Nancy's reaction. "There's some kind of connection between Boris's murder and Raskol's. Two murders on two continents involving members of the same family—that's no coincidence."

"Assassination," Frank said. "That might be another strong reason for Cass to turn down the crown."

"He certainly doesn't want to be next," murmured Nancy as if lost in another time. Then she snapped her head up and came back to the present. "You think he's so afraid of becoming king that he'd kill someone?" Nancy shook her head. "I met Cass. He didn't seem the type—"

"Come on, Nancy," Frank argued. "We've all met people who have seemed to be perfectly nice, and they turned out to be murderers."

Nancy gave in with just a shrug.

"Okay, Nancy Drew, I want to know what's going on," Joe demanded.

Frank and Nancy stared at him in amazement.

"You're not following this conversation very well, and you keep coming up with information I don't believe I've heard before," Joe charged her.

"What are you talking about?" Frank asked Joe, but he kept his eyes on Nancy. She was turning a little pink.

"So, Cass is not from Panaslava," Joe pointed out. "How do we know that? He has a French passport, but maybe he went to France from Panaslava. You seem to know differently."

"Uh," Nancy began.

"Wait, I'm not done," Joe said. "How do you *know* that Cass won't go back to Paris? You seem to know it, while we're just theorizing."

"Joe," Nancy said, putting a hand on his arm. "Frank, I'm sorry. I really wanted to talk to Bess first."

"What happened, Nancy?" Joe asked gently, seeing that she was genuinely upset.

"When I was in the Marvins' house and Bess's mom was outside giving that photographer what for, the phone rang. I answered it. It was Cass, and he mistook me for Bess at first."

"What did he say?" Frank asked excitedly.

"Basically just what I let slip here," she answered. "He said he was King Boris's son and that his father raised him on delusions of returning to rule Panaslava. But he doesn't want any part of it. He also said that he didn't kill Raskol, but before he could explain what happened, he heard police sirens and got scared. He hung up."

"And he didn't tell you where he was hiding?" Frank asked.

"No." Nancy shook her head. "If he had, I think I would have had to tell Chief McGinnis. As it is, I don't know whether I've made a mistake not telling him about the phone call. Fortunately, he'd already found out the truth about Cass's identity."

"Lucky for you," Joe said. "But why not tell him about the phone call?"

Frank jumped in at this point. "What would Chief McGinnis do if he knew Cass had called Bess, Joe?"

A lightbulb may as well have appeared over Joe's head. "He'd find Bess and set her up to give Cass away next time he tried to reach her," Joe said.

"Very good." Frank slapped his brother on the top of his head.

"Wait," Nancy cried. "I just remembered the

most important thing he said—that *he* was now a target!"

"Unfortunately, that doesn't let Cass off the hook. He still has two motives to kill Raskol," Joe said. "He doesn't want to be next in line for the crown, and he certainly doesn't want to be next in line on any assassin's hit list."

Joe shook his head. "The question is this: Is Casimir 'Cass Carroll' Karolyi Ladinovic the kind of man who would kill to ensure his privacy?"

Chapter

Fifteen

THEIR CONVERSATION HAD ruined Nancy's appetite. No matter how she argued against the Hardys' theories of Cass as a killer, she kept tripping over one fact. Cass wouldn't come in and face the accusations against him. That looked bad and only got worse the longer he remained a fugitive.

When Egon came by with a tray of desserts, he had a hard time tempting her. He acted so woebegone at her refusal, Nancy forced herself to nibble on a pastry, but she didn't enjoy it.

Nancy felt sympathy for the young prince in trouble. But she was completely heartsick over what Cass's situation was doing to Bess. Not only was Bess's mystery man very different from the guy she had imagined him to be, but he might turn out to be a murderer.

Be honest, a little voice in the back of Nancy's head scolded. You wouldn't be so sure Cass was innocent if Bess wasn't involved with him. The case is pretty strong against him.

Nancy suddenly felt dreadfully tired. It seemed as if a week had gone by since she had eaten Hannah's pancakes that morning.

"I have to get home, guys," she said. "What time is it, anyway?"

Joe and Frank simultaneously looked at their watches. Although she was beat, Nancy noticed with amusement that Joe wore a high-tech digital watch with all kinds of LCD readouts and buttons to push, while Frank had a simple gold analog watch with a worn brown leather strap.

"Eleven o'clock," Frank said.

"Eleven-oh-two," Joe countered.

Nancy moaned. "I can't possibly go see Bess now. I'm too tired."

Egon met them at the door on their way out. As he held the door for Nancy, he bent toward her ear and said a few words that Nancy didn't understand. She looked at him quizzically.

"Just a blessing from an old Zelenogoran *grof*," Egon said with a smile. "I think we all need a little luck on our side right now."

"Bed," Nancy said aloud as she pulled onto her block. "That's all I want right now. Crawl under the covers and forget all about this mess for a while."

"Welcome back," Hannah Gruen said, opening the door as Nancy inserted her key. "The phone's been ringing off the hook for you." Hannah pointed to a small pile of message notes neatly stacked by the hall telephone. "I'm making tea. Would you like some?"

"No, but thanks, Hannah." Nancy rifled through the notes. "Brenda Carlton, Brenda Carlton, Brenda Carlton . . . George Fayne. Sorry, Brenda, it's past my bedtime." She looked at Hannah. "It's not too late to call George back, is it?"

Hannah raised her eyebrows. "We're still up, aren't we?"

Nancy punched the speed-dial code for George, who answered on the first ring.

"Hey, George, it's Nancy. Am I calling too late? I was out with Frank and Joe and just came in the door."

"No problem," George answered. "Aunt Anna said you three had been over there."

There was an uneasy silence. Nancy got the sense that George was upset.

"So," George began hesitantly. "I guess you know that Bess is staying with us."

"Right," Nancy said lamely. "How is she? Can I speak to her?"

"That's what I wanted to talk to *you* about." George's voice got softer, and the tension seemed to slide away. "She's barely said a word all day. She's just dragged herself off to bed. That's not the Bess Marvin we both know and love. I would have had to hold *that* Bess back from taking a running dive into the center ring of this media circus."

"I wouldn't go that far," Nancy said. "Bess may thrive on attention, but she's less than fond of Brenda Carlton."

"Brenda?" George repeated. "What are you talking about?"

"I'm talking about the fact that Brenda is trying to interview Bess. That's why Bess and Mr. Marvin sneaked over to your house, isn't it?"

"That's the least of our problems. Brenda Carlton is nothing compared to the circus going on around here," George replied.

"Oh, no, what's happening now?" Nancy asked, her voice weary and concerned.

"Haven't you been watching the news? Well, since you just got home, I guess you haven't. Switch on one of the local stations. The newscasts are still running."

Nancy turned on the television and tuned in the River Heights stations. The late news was almost finished. The anchorman with the perfect teeth turned to his pretty blond partner and said, "So, Kristin, why don't you give the recap of tonight's stories?"

Aiming a dazzling smile at the camera, Kristin started talking. She was obviously reading straight off the TelePrompTer. "There is a startling development in the Raskol murder case. Sources close to the investigation revealed that not only was Pavel Raskol a messenger for the assassinated King Boris of Panaslava, but the prime suspect for Raskol's murder is the fugitive crown prince of that exiled royal family. At this time the police seem to be focusing their search for the suspect in the neighborhood of Little Panaslava."

Nancy gasped so deeply, she almost choked. "This is awful! I didn't want Bess to find out this way. I meant to talk to her first."

"Too late for that," George said.

"How did she take it?" Nancy asked, dreading the answer.

"Well, normally, you'd expect her to be all over this, like a bee on honey," George said. "Instead, she just sat there, perfectly quiet. I wound up channel-hopping to see if other newscasts were covering the same story. They were. But Bess didn't stay to watch. She just excused herself and went up to her room. To cry, I think."

Nancy felt terrible. "You tell her I'll be right over—"

"Don't bother, Nancy," George replied. "She isn't talking to anyone, and from what little she described of your outing together, I think you might be the last person she'd like to see right now."

Nancy was afraid of that. "It's that bad?"

There was a pause. "Yeah, I'd say so," George said. "But look"—she launched into the sentence with a brighter voice—"you go to bed. You and Bess both need to sleep on this. We'll have a little powwow in the morning. Okay?"

"I'll be over first thing," Nancy promised, and hung up the phone.

When Nancy finally did get under the covers, it took her a long time to fall asleep.

The next morning she was up before the sun. She showered quickly and threw on one of her favorite detective outfits: jeans and a handknit white Aran Island sweater. She sat down with a bowl of cereal in front of the early edition of the news on television. Nancy wanted to be as well informed as Bess before she went to see her. What is this day going to bring? she wondered.

Every channel—local and national—was covering some part of what was now being called "A Royal Case of Murder." Since the story had broken the night before, the networks had moved news teams to River Heights, backing up their local affiliates.

It was a weird feeling to see national news celebrities standing in front of various locales in Little Panaslava. Channel 2 was obviously courting a young audience by placing a live reporter inside the club where Nancy had met Cass. Channel 3 had positioned a young woman outside Egon's café to interview Egon himself, while Channel 6 was covering the front of the nondescript house where Cass had rented his room.

Nancy breathed a sigh of relief that none of these newshounds was banging on Bess's door.

At that moment the doorbell rang. Hannah appeared just as Nancy was getting to her feet.

"It's for you, Nancy," she called. "Your friends from Bayport."

Hannah led the Hardys in. "Could I get you boys something to eat? Coffee? An English muffin, perhaps?"

"I wouldn't say no," Joe responded with a grin.

"Nothing for me, thank you, Hannah," his brother replied.

The Hardys joined Nancy on the couch in front of the TV.

Frank rolled his eyes. "Don't you ever stop eating?" he asked his younger brother, but he didn't allow him time to answer. He turned to Nancy. "The Bottomless Pit here and I decided to get out of our hotel before Bascomb came to scream at us again. He was in a bad enough mood last night over Joe's sticking him with Brenda."

"Bad mood?" Joe said. "He burst into our room ready to skin us alive with a dull knife!"

"I think he was jealous that we knew before he did that Cass Carroll is really a prince," Frank explained.

"What makes it hurt is that he thinks we told Brenda Carlton." Joe acted disgusted. "How did he put it? He needs people who won't 'spill their guts whenever some bimbo with a press card comes wiggling by.'"

Nancy wrapped her arms around her stomach. "Please, I don't want to go there this early in the morning."

Frank grinned. "Just back us up on this, Nancy. Bascomb thinks Brenda sank her hooks into us after we left McGinnis's office. But we were out to dinner, right?"

"We certainly were," Nancy concurred. "As I recall, you"—she pointed at Frank—"ate Thumper, and you"—she pointed at Joe—"ate Bambi."

Frank began to protest, when Joe caught their attention.

"Uh-oh!" Joe nodded toward the television screen. "Here are some new shots from the royal family album."

Pictures of Prince Casimir were being sent all over the wires and were broadcast in mere minutes from sites all over Europe.

The young man in the photos was definitely Cass Carroll, though his hair was shorter and he wasn't quite so lean. The photos showed not only the prince but his lifestyle, too. So far this morning, Nancy had seen Cass leaving a hot Paris nightclub in a tuxedo, arriving at the Ascot races, and cruising with some fortunate royal relatives who still had their titles. Now Channel 3 had found a picture of Cass on a beach in the Riviera, with a bikini-clad girl on each arm.

"I'm beginning to see some advantages in this prince thing," Joe said with a long look at the screen. He frowned as the station switched back to the anchor team's desk.

"Don't worry, Joe," Nancy offered. *Babewatch* will be on soon."

But Nancy hushed Frank's laughter as she caught what the anchorman was saying.

"We've got a new development in the royal murder case. Leo Pekary, the Chicago businessman with strong ties to the former Panaslav republics, has arrived in River Heights and is calling a press conference."

Behind the announcer, a picture of Leo Pekary came into view. It was obviously a stock photo, hastily pulled from the news bureau's files. The image showed a bull-necked, gray-haired man with a badly mended broken nose and heavy eyebrows. His big, determined jaw shone blue, as if no amount of shaving could make the stubble go away. The man's shrewd eyes seemed to peer out of the screen, directly at Nancy. His lips were surprisingly expressive, twisted as if he were about to crack a joke.

"Pekary came to this country as a Panaslavan immigrant more than thirty years ago," the announcer continued. "In that time he turned a small trucking company into a worldwide transportation conglomerate. He was the head of the American-Panaslavan International Chamber of Commerce and has always stood as a spokesman for Panaslavan interests in this country. His Panaslav Foundation has donated generously for humanitarian aid to the newly formed republics. You may also remember that he was active in the recent Sarabian elections."

"*That's* where I've seen him before!" Frank said. "He tried to run for president of Sarabia but wound up being a major backer of one of the parties in the parliament. His face kept popping up in the newspapers."

"And occasionally on TV," Nancy added, "the rare times the networks were paying any attention to the area before the shooting began."

Joe shrugged. "He looks like a criminal to me."

The TV newsman was looking at someone off-camera and nodding. "And now we go to John O'Rourke on the streets of River Heights."

"Thanks, Tom." A stiff breeze was ruffling the news reporter's usually perfect hair. "We're standing outside the local offices of the Panaslavan Foundation here on Janocek Avenue."

Nancy noticed that the out-of-towner pronounced *Janocek* "Jan-o-seck" instead of "Yahn-o-check."

"Mr. Pekary is apparently very concerned over the tragedies that have occurred within the Panaslavan royal family. King Boris, who was assassinated two days ago, was involved in behind-the-scenes peace negotiations—oh! Here comes Mr. Pekary now!" The camera switched to the street.

A chauffeured Mercedes rolled to a stop. Leo Pekary opened his own door and stepped out to meet the sudden rush of media reporters and cameramen who advanced on him.

Frank looked impressed. "He must have some pull, to get all the networks and cable news organizations to come to him."

Nancy shushed him and leaned closer to the screen. Pekary looked a little older than his photograph. Maybe it was the look of concern on his face that aged him. He walked deliberately to a small podium that had a microphone set up on it. Leo Pekary adjusted the height of the mike, cleared his throat, and began to speak.

"Two days ago the cause of peace in Panaslava suffered a terrible blow when a cowardly gunman shot down Boris Ladinovic. This brave man displayed the same greatness and wisdom his ancestors showed when they ruled in Panaslava, talking to representatives of the various factions in the region, trying to lead them to negotiations. Every Panaslavan of goodwill must mourn his passing.

"And our burden of grief becomes all the heavier when we learn that Boris's son, Casimir Ladinovic, is a fugitive here in the United States, suspected of murder. I'm here in River Heights today to offer any help I can in this sad matter, as I would try to help any fellow Panaslavan. That's why I make this personal appeal."

Pekary spread his hands in a pleading gesture and looked directly into the cameras. "Prince Casimir, please, go to the police—or come here." Pekary gestured to the offices of the foundation. His presence was very commanding. He had the press—and probably the television audience—hanging on every word he said.

"We will make the arrangements with the authorities and ensure you have the best legal representation. I speak as a friend and as a respectful associate of your father. I personally pledge every penny I have to your defense. Thank you. That's all I have to say."

The television people immediately bombarded Pekary with questions, but he waved them back with a smile, shaking his head.

"Well, that was unexpected," Frank said.

Joe shoved his hands in his pockets. He glanced off toward the kitchen. "Maybe I should go and see how that English muffin is coming along."

"Yeah, do that," Frank said, and rolled his eyes. "What do you think about Pekary's offer, Nancy?"

Nancy turned off the television, cutting off the anchorman's recap of the press conference in midword. "I don't know what good it does, except that it was great free publicity for Leo Pekary and his foundation."

Frank shook his head. "And it ups the pressure on Cass. If he doesn't take Pekary's offer, he'll look even more guilty."

Nancy jumped to her feet and began to pace the room. "But if Cass takes the offer, he'll be stuck in prison, a perfect target for the Haiduk, just as his father was . . ."

Frank's eyes went wide, and he grabbed Nancy's hand. "Did you hear what you just said? A target for the Haiduk! That *has* to be why the Haiduk was sent to River Heights! He's the second half of a one-two punch."

Nancy nodded as a chill spread through her.

"Aimed to wipe out the royal heirs of the Ladinovic line!" Frank whispered in awe.

"I have to see Bess," Nancy said. "If the media talks to her, or even mentions her, the Haiduk will know exactly how to get to Cass."

Frank put Nancy's fear into words precisely. "Through Bess."

Chapter

Sixteen

J OE!" FRANK HARDY RUSHED into the kitchen. "Swallow whatever you've got in your mouth, and leave the rest! We've got to get downtown to police headquarters."

"Mish mettuh me mem-paudant," Joe complained. He swallowed and repeated, "This better be important."

"It is," Frank assured his brother. "I think we've just figured out who the Haiduk is after—and Bess may be in danger."

"Beff?" Joe repeated as he tried to down the rest of his English muffin in one bite.

When Joe heard the theory that Frank and Nancy had come up with, he wrapped the second half of his muffin in a napkin and put it into his pocket, thanked Hannah, and took off out the door before Nancy and Frank.

"I've got to go straight to George's to see Bess," Nancy declared. "You two go see the chief and Bascomb. Then get to George's as fast as you can—unless something comes up. You have her phone number?"

"You bet," Frank replied. "Be careful, Nancy. We don't know who the Haiduk is or just how much he knows."

"Double ditto to you guys," she replied.

Frank and Joe got into their rental car. Nancy took her own car. At the corner they went their separate ways.

Joe drove while Frank went over Nancy's revelation about the Haiduk's probable victim again. They headed for Judiciary Square—and the police station—as fast as the law would allow.

After he was satisfied that he could find no holes in their theory, Frank tapped his fingers impatiently on the dashboard, nervously breaking the silence.

"Now, Frank," Joe scolded him with a grin, "you wouldn't want me to speed."

Joe parked as close to the police station as he could without using a handicapped slot, which, as he pointed out to Frank, would have been illegal. They locked the car and dashed into police headquarters.

"Well," Chuck Bascomb, the State Department man, said nastily, "if it isn't the Leaky Brothers."

"Stow it, Bascomb," Frank said. "We don't

know who gave away Cass Carroll's royal origins, but we know it wasn't Nancy, and it sure wasn't us."

Bascomb glared at them through slitted eyes. "How reassuring, but the sad fact is, you've let yourselves get sidetracked by the Carroll investigation instead of paying attention to the reason we're here."

"That's what you think," Joe replied angrily. "Cass Carroll *is* the reason we're here."

Bascomb gave him a hard look. "You two should be stage comedians," he said in a stony voice. "Have you gone back to your theory that Casimir Ladinovic is the Haiduk in disguise?"

Frank watched his brother's face go red. But, admirably, Joe restrained himself.

"You explain it," Joe said tightly, turning to Frank.

"Maybe we should see if Chief McGinnis is available, too," Frank suggested.

Bascomb raised a hand. "Not until I've heard this so-called theory." He scrutinized the brothers. "Go for it."

As Frank tried to reenact—with Joe's help—how Nancy and he had come up with their idea that the Haiduk was after Cass, Bascomb's frown got deeper and deeper.

"This is totally ridiculous," he said.

"As ridiculous as Nancy's theory that Cass was a Ladinovic?" Frank asked. "That was a ridiculous theory that just happened to turn out to be correct."

"The one sure thing in this Haiduk situation is that the assassination is political, connected with the present situation in the former Panaslav republics." Bascomb gave them his most authoritative glare. "The old royal family is a dead letter in today's politics."

"That's not what Leo Pekary just said on the news," Frank shot back. "According to him, King Boris was conducting secret meetings between the factions, trying to hammer out some kind of peace."

"Pekary." Bascomb sneered. "What can you say about a private citizen who tries to run the world's foreign policy?"

"Spoken like a true foreign service official," Chief McGinnis said with a smile, appearing behind Frank and Joe. "Who's got you so annoyed?"

"Leo Pekary," Frank replied, while Bascomb was still busy sneering. "Did you know he's in town?"

"Do I ever!" The chief groaned. "I've been in the mayor's office since dawn ironing out security for his visit. We've had an easier time with United States presidents coming through."

"Did you catch any of his press conference?" Frank asked. "He said that King Boris was assassinated because he was leading a secret peace effort in Panaslava. That started us wondering whether our assassin was after a Ladinovic on this side of the Atlantic."

"You mean Prince Casimir?" McGinnis said, intrigued.

"It's a preposterous idea, McGinnis," Bascomb blustered. "It completely ignores the murder of Pavel Raskol—or are you all going back to the idea that he's the Haiduk? One thing is sure: it couldn't be a case of mistaken identity. Raskol was a middle-aged man who looked nothing at all like Casimir Ladinovic. Or maybe we have a *blind* assassin? That would explain everything."

Now it was the chief's turn to become furious.

Frank leaped in, just in case the chief had to worry about his blood pressure. "Suppose, just suppose, it was a case of being in the wrong place at the wrong time."

"Aw, come on!" Bascomb stood up impatiently. "This isn't a TV cop show."

Frank didn't miss a beat. "Grant me, just for a moment, that Cass was the Haiduk's target," he said. "The assassin makes his move at the River View Motel. Raskol gets in the way of the knife. Is it really that far-fetched?"

Bascomb shook his head impatiently. "The Haiduk is a professional. If he'd been following Ladinovic, he wouldn't have made a move with a witness around."

Frank shrugged. "Maybe he spotted Cass with Raskol and wanted to get the job done quickly."

"Suppose. Maybe." Bascomb sounded disgusted. "You kids may be hotshots, but I think you've been watching too many movies. Let me tell you something—real life isn't neat and convenient."

"Our Haiduk theory would also explain why Raskol died . . . and give Ladinovic a strong—and innocent—motive to stay in hiding," Frank continued, as if Bascomb hadn't said a word.

"Fear of capture for having murdered a man is a motive for hiding as well," Bascomb countered.

"But what would be Cass's motive for murdering Raskol?" Joe picked up the defense, directing his comments to Chief McGinnis. "If Raskol was asking Cass to come back to Paris to see his dying father, he was too late. If he wanted Cass to return to Paris and be crowned king, all Cass had to do was refuse. The only possible reason Cass could have for killing Raskol was that Raskol himself had killed King Boris and was attacking Cass."

Joe glanced at Bascomb. "We know your feelings on Raskol being an assassin. But if it *were* the case, Cass would have been acting in self-defense. No, the only theory that covers all the facts in Raskol's death is an assassination attempt on Cass gone wrong."

Chief McGinnis nodded. "I think it's at least a possibility," he said, and then cleared his throat. "It does address both of our problems."

Frank saw Bascomb's face change as the chief weighed in on their side. "Of course, it's a *possibility*," he admitted. "Anything's possible. But there's only one way we'll ever know what happened to Raskol. Whether he was the killer or simply a witness, Casimir Ladinovic was there. He'll have to surrender to us so that he can be questioned."

Frank and Joe exchanged a glance. "If Cass gives himself up, then the Haiduk will know exactly where to find him," Frank said.

"That should not even be a consideration," Bascomb huffed. "We can put him in protective custody."

"Sounds great," Joe said. "Would that mean solitary confinement in jail, or will you hide him in a hotel room for the rest of his life?"

"Which may be pretty short, if this Haiduk guy is as good as you say he is," Frank added.

Chief McGinnis gave Frank and Joe a hard look. "You boys seem to have an insultingly low opinion of the River Heights Police Department."

Frank put up his hands in surrender. "No such thing, Chief. But the Haiduk isn't just a killer, or an organized crime hit man. We're talking about a KGB-trained assassin who's spent a career in state-sponsored terrorism. I wonder if any local police force could stop him."

McGinnis nodded as if his neck hurt. "Point taken," he said reluctantly. "But it's all 'what if's' and 'maybes' until—*unless*—Prince Casimir turns himself in."

Joe spoke up. "Is he likely to turn himself in without some assurances that he'll be safe?"

"The kid is still a murder suspect," Bascomb

said. "I don't see any use contacting the FBI or other agencies until he comes in to explain what happened the night Raskol was murdered."

"Which could get him killed," Frank stated in frustration. He turned to Bascomb. "As a State Department man, don't you think it's worth a little more effort to try to save the Panaslav peace negotiations?"

"Those negotiations died with King Boris," Bascomb replied coldly.

"Great," Frank snapped. "So it's immaterial to you whether Cass dies or not."

"Okay, okay, calm down," Chief McGinnis ordered in his official voice. "You've told us your idea. I'll keep it in mind, but we still have a fugitive out there. Whether he's a perpetrator or a victim, we won't know until he comes in. And we can't address his safety concerns until he contacts us. So we're still where we were when we started this near brawl."

No one had anything more to say.

"I suggest we all get back to work," the chief said. Then he turned and walked toward his office. Without turning back, he yelled, "Now!" then slammed his office door shut behind him.

Frank and Joe lit out of there. They had no desire to exchange another word with the State Department agent who'd brought them to River Heights in the first place.

As Frank got in the driver's side, Joe spoke up. "Do you remember how to get to George's?"

"No," Frank said. "Do you?"

"Yes, I do," Joe replied.

After a long pause, Frank asked Joe, "Do you want to drive?"

"Yes, I do," Joe replied.

They silently got back out of the car. Joe walked around the front, and Frank walked around the back. They both got back into the car. As soon as Joe started the engine, the two of them burst out laughing at themselves.

"I noticed one thing," Frank said as they got under way. "Ol' Bascomb changed his tune pretty fast after Chief McGinnis got interested in our theory."

Joe grinned. "Let's just hope we don't have to come up with any more really good theories."

When they arrived at George's house, Joe pulled in behind a very big Mercedes-Benz. "Looks like they're having fancy company," Joe commented. "Unless Brenda Carlton borrowed Daddy's car."

Frank scanned the area but saw only Nancy's car parked at the curb. There was no trace of the girl reporter or her red car.

The Faynes did have company, someone Frank would never have expected—Leo Pekary. It didn't look as if they'd get a chance to catch up with Nancy anytime soon.

"I'm pleased to meet you both," the bigwig said when Frank and Joe were introduced.

He's got a politician's easy manners, Frank thought—and perfect campaign clothes, judging by the casual but expensive jacket and slacks that Pekary had worn for his press conference.

Then something else struck Frank. Pekary must have an amazing organization in River Heights. He'd just arrived in town, and he knew not only that Bess was going out with Cass but also that Bess was hiding out at her cousin's house.

"I hope you'll all help by joining in with my request to this young lady." Pekary gestured to an unexpectedly tight-lipped Bess, who was sitting alone on the couch. Nancy and George stood behind her, with Mr. and Mrs. Fayne in armchairs to her left. Bess's parents weren't in evidence.

"Perhaps you don't know, but I came to River Heights to make a public appeal to Prince Casimir to give himself up. I promised to mount the best defense possible out of my own funds."

"We saw the press conference," Frank said.

"You made him sound like a murderer!" Bess shouted. From the startled expressions on the faces all around, this was the first thing Bess had said to Leo Pekary.

Pekary didn't react but answered only as if they were continuing a conversation.

"If he can clear himself, all the better," he said. "But he must do it *quickly,* or people will think he has a guilty conscience."

"He's not guilty of anything!" Bess shouted back.

"But you must admit, that's what people will

believe if he keeps hiding. If he's innocent, why not come forward?" Pekary's tone was warm and reasonable, in contrast to his thuglike looks.

Bess obviously wanted to smack him. "No big deal. All he has to do is trust you," she said sarcastically. "He doesn't even know you."

"True. Although I did work with his father, Prince Casimir doesn't know me," Pekary admitted. "I thought that if he heard my appeal spoken by someone he knows and trusts—"

"So now you want him to trust me to trust you," Bess said grimly.

Leo Pekary turned to George's parents. "I know I'll have to clear this with Ms. Marvin's parents," he said, with all the persuasiveness of a TV commercial announcer. "It might be difficult for her to deal with the publicity that would naturally result from appearing on television . . ."

Joe choked back a laugh.

Frank gave his brother a dirty look but had to admit that Joe had a point. Bess Marvin was hardly what he'd call the shy, retiring type. Rather, he knew that she was a TV talk-show host wannabe. Judging from his performance that morning, Pekary had sized her up pretty accurately. He was talking about putting her on all the TV networks. That struck Frank as a very clever bribe. The Bess they normally knew should be delighted to dive into that national spotlight.

But the Bess sitting on the couch only stared

down at her hands, which were tightly clasped in her lap. "I—I don't think I could," she replied. Her voice was so soft that Frank had to strain to hear.

Something is going on with Bess, he thought.

Leo Pekary met Bess's pronouncement with silence. He seemed pretty angry but only for an instant. Then, like the good public figure he was, he somehow swallowed his feelings and gave Bess a reasonably pleasant smile.

"I know it's a lot to ask of anyone. Please be assured that I'll do everything in my power to help Casimir in the way of bail. I'll ensure your access to him. You can even use my car and driver."

He's really piling it on, Frank thought. But is Bess going to buy what he's selling?

Pekary stretched a hand to her, almost as if he were pleading. "Perhaps if you took a little time to consider . . ."

Bess physically shut him out while sitting perfectly still on the couch. She shook her head. "I don't think I could do that," she stated.

Pekary turned to the adults, then to the young people in the room for support. When no one else spoke, he shrugged.

Bess stayed on the couch as the others saw Leo Pekary to the door.

The businessman strode off to his Mercedes, which now had a driver in the front seat.

Frank's eyebrows rose. Where had that guy been when we pulled up? he wondered.

Any guesses he might have made were interrupted by the sharp intake of breath beside him.

Frank turned. "Something wrong, Nancy? Hey!" He hadn't been ready for Nancy to grab his arm and drag him out the front door.

He glanced back at Joe, who followed his stumbling brother to the street.

"Nancy? What—what are you doing?" Frank tried to pull back as Nancy hauled him forward. "More importantly, *why?*"

"Didn't you see the driver in that Mercedes?" Nancy demanded.

"For about two seconds."

Nancy tugged on his arm again. "I think it was Tad Vlachovic!"

Chapter

Seventeen

ARE YOU SURE it was Vlachovic driving Pekary's car?" Frank asked as Nancy quickened her pace, not letting go of Frank's arm.

"No," Nancy admitted. "I only got a glimpse of cropped blond hair and a flash of his profile." The Mercedes was at the corner, making a right turn. Nancy broke into a run. "My car," she said, hauling Frank with her, Joe right behind them.

They piled into Nancy's Mustang, and Frank barely had his door closed before Nancy tore off. "So why the big chase?" he asked.

"Frank, did you forget your Wheaties this morning? If Tad Vlachovic, Mr. Street Thug of Little Panaslava, is driving Leo Pekary's car, what does that say about Pekary?" Nancy barely stopped at the corner before turning right.

"What did you think of Pekary in there?" Joe leaned forward in the backseat to ask.

"He was very persuasive, made lots of promises, some outright and others just hinted at . . ." Frank's voice ran down.

"But?" Nancy prompted.

"But I didn't trust him," Frank admitted.

"I couldn't get a handle on him, either during his press conference or at the Fayne house," Nancy said. "But if he hires guys like Tad Vlachovic, then the bad feeling I get isn't just instinct."

At the corner Nancy checked in all four directions. "I don't see them."

"There," Frank said suddenly. "Three blocks ahead. They're making a right."

Nancy reached the corner where the Mercedes had turned and spun the wheel to the right. Her car went into the turn faster than she would have liked.

Then there was a sound like a shot, and all at once the car seemed to be driving itself—straight toward a street lamp!

Nancy fought all the worst driver's instincts—to stomp on the brakes and fight the wheel. Instead, she feathered the brakes gently and turned into the skid. After a bad moment, she managed to gain control of the car. They didn't hit the lamp; they didn't even climb the curb. They just made a long curve along the empty street and came to a stop.

Frank let go of a long-held breath. "Nice driving," he complimented her.

"Thanks," Nancy said, pressing her foot hard on the gas. There was no mistaking the sound, the *wubbiddy-wubbiddy-wub* coming from her front right tire.

"They say that timing is everything," she grumbled. "All I can say is, what a time for a flat."

The three of them stared out the windshield, watching the Mercedes disappear in the distance.

Nancy slowly pulled to the side of the street, got out, and walked around to the suspicious-sounding tire. Frank stood beside her, surveying the damage. Joe didn't even bother looking. He reached down beside the driver's seat and popped the trunk.

Twenty minutes later, when the spare was in place, Joe said, "Here's the cause of your trouble." Joe tilted the tire he'd just removed toward Nancy. She caught a little greenish glint in one of the outer treads. On closer inspection, she saw it was a piece of glass.

"Looks like it came from a bottle," Joe surmised. "At least you can be fairly sure that Tad Vlachovic didn't shoot your tire out."

"True," Nancy said grimly. "But he could have sabotaged it just the same."

Frank frowned. "I know you don't like the guy, but don't you think you're jumping to conclusions?"

"Like the guy?" Nancy repeated Frank's choice of words incredulously. "You haven't been trapped in a dark alley with him coming after you."

"Everyone calm down," Joe said, stepping between the two like a referee. "How likely do you think it is that there'd be broken glass—much less a broken bottle—in front of George Fayne's house?"

When they got back to George's house, Nancy parked where the Mercedes had been. She immediately got out and began searching.

Joe and Frank joined her as she crouched along the curb. "Find anything?" Joe asked.

"Just what I expected to find," Nancy answered. "Nothing. There's no glass here."

Frank gave her a hand up, but she could tell he still wasn't going along with her sabotage theory. "You know, Nancy, you've been spending a lot of time in Little Panaslava," he said. "I saw a lot of broken glass in the streets there. A piece might have gotten caught in the tread and started a slow leak, which only blew the tire when you took that wild corner."

Nancy felt her face grow warm as Frank continued. "It makes more sense than believing that Tad Vlachovic carries a broken bottle around to sabotage his enemies' cars."

Biting her lip, Nancy gave him a brief, jerky nod. "You may be right," she admitted grudgingly.

"Then again," Joe piped up, "he might be wrong, and you might be right."

"Thanks for your confidence, Joe," Nancy said, smiling warmly. "It's nice to have someone's support."

"Yeah, Joe," Frank growled. "Thanks."

"What has gotten into you two?" Joe asked. "Either way, Nancy got a flat tire, and we couldn't find out if Tad was behind the wheel of Pekary's car. But we know he might be involved, so we'll keep an eye out for him. Okay?"

Nancy knew what her problem was: Bess. "Bess refused to talk to me this morning. I didn't even get to see her until Pekary showed up."

"You haven't talked to her since before she jumped out of your car?" Joe asked.

Nancy shook her head.

Frank took Nancy's right arm, and Joe took her left, and together they marched her up to the Faynes' front door. It was closed and locked against any media intruders who might have discovered Bess's hiding place. Frank rang the bell.

"Everything all right?" George asked when she answered the door. "You sure left in a hurry."

"I thought I saw Tad Vlachovic driving Mr. Pekary's car," Nancy replied in a low voice.

George's eyebrows shot up. "How would a lowlife like that end up working for such a bigshot?"

"I'm not sure it was Tad. That's why I tried to follow them. I wanted to get a better look."

Nancy scowled. "Instead, all I got was a flat tire."

George frowned. "If it *was* that Vlachovic guy—well, I'm not thrilled that he knows where I live." She hesitated for a moment. "Do you want to try to talk to Bess again? I think she might be ready."

Nancy took a deep breath. "Lead the way."

Bess was the cheeriest friend Nancy had— definitely the fun-now-worry-later type. She was flirtatious, a little silly sometimes, and always loved being the center of attention. This new, serious, even morose Bess was scary. She certainly hadn't been her usual self during Leo Pekary's visit.

What was wrong? There had to be something more going on here than fallout from their argument. Even an argument over a boy Bess was crazy about.

Bess was still sitting hunched over on the sofa. She looked up at her four friends and lowered her head to stare back into her lap. "I thought you guys had gone," she said grumpily.

It's a start, Nancy thought.

"And we're really glad to see you, too," Joe shot back, flopping onto a chair.

George suddenly exploded. "Look, Bess Marvin, I'm not going to let you pull this anymore. Don't talk to reporters, if you don't want to, fine. But don't play the prima donna with us. It's been like pulling teeth to get a word out of you since last night."

"What happened last night?" Nancy asked.

"Nothing—as far as I know." George glared at her cousin. "Bess, if we did something to upset you, tell us. Please."

Bess raised her head, and her blue eyes blazed for a second, but she said nothing.

"Wait, George," Nancy said. "I don't blame Bess for not talking to me." She sat down next to her friend and spoke softly. "I owe you an apology, Bess. I shouldn't have let you go after our fight. I should have at least come back later to talk. I'm sorry."

There was no response.

"Bess?" Nancy asked. "Will you say something?"

It wasn't Bess but George who broke the silence. "It's not that, Nancy. Bess and I talked it over when she got here yesterday. She was angry, sure, but she admitted that she'd overreacted. She was fine by dinner. It was later. Something made her start behaving like this, but I don't think it had anything to do with you."

Nancy turned back to Bess and studied her long and hard. "You remind me of someone right now," she said. "Cass Carroll. Remember how you felt when he was keeping secrets from you?"

Her comment was little more than a shot in the dark, but it seemed right on target. Bess jumped as if someone had stuck her with a pin. Her shoulders straightened, and her lips began to quiver.

"I—I'm sorry, George, Nancy . . . I guess I

really have been a pain. It's just all that's happened—"

George dropped onto the sofa and flung an arm around Bess's shoulders. "Hey, you don't have to face it alone. You've got friends. Nancy and I will do anything we can to help. Right, Nan?"

"Sure thing," Nancy promised.

"Hey, what about us?" Joe asked. "We'll do whatever we can, too."

Even as Bess began to open up just a little, Nancy continued to see a guarded look in her friend's eyes. *Bess knows something she's not telling, and she's afraid we'll make her tell.*

A small voice scolded Nancy from the back of her brain. *You're thinking like a detective. This isn't a suspect—this is one of your best friends.*

Nancy sighed, feeling guilty. "I think we'd better give your parents a call, Bess," she finally said. "Mr. Pekary managed to track you down almost as soon as he arrived in River Heights. He didn't drag the media along with him, but I expect it won't be too long before press people figure out where you are."

That got a reaction from Bess. She jumped to her feet and stalked around the room. "I'm not talking to Brenda Carlton. I'm not talking to *anybody!*"

George dialed the Marvins' number and handed the phone over to Bess. When Bess hung up, Nancy offered her a lift home.

"Maybe I can get her to talk in the car," Nancy whispered to George while Bess was packing her things.

George and her parents waved goodbye from the front door, and Frank and Joe waved before they drove away to find some lunch. Bess hardly reacted.

This is so weird, Nancy thought, her detective senses going into overdrive. Bess was never very good at hiding anything, but she was working hard at it now.

All at once, it hit Nancy—she knew what Bess was hiding. Nancy kept her eyes on the road as she asked her question. "What did you do, tell George it was a wrong number when Cass called?"

Bess made a noise somewhere between a choke and a sob. When Nancy glanced over, she saw that her friend's eyes were full of tears.

"How?" Bess couldn't get another word out.

"He called your house when I was there, and I picked up the phone." Nancy shook her head. "I think I told him where you were. The Faynes' number is listed in the phone book."

"Yes. Cass called." Bess's voice came out a shaky hiss. "He gave me the number of a pay phone and told me to call him back. He told me what happened. He's not a murderer, Nancy."

"On the contrary, Bess, I think someone wants to murder him."

"That's what Cass said. Raskol had warned him, telling him to watch out." Bess stared at Nancy for a minute before bursting into tears. "I just can't carry what I know around all alone anymore."

Nancy pulled over and stopped, letting her friend cry until she seemed to be cried out.

"Do you want to start at the beginning?" Nancy asked.

"Cass ran out of Egon's place because he wanted to be alone after hearing that his father had been killed. He said he couldn't believe it when he ran into Pavel Raskol. Cass had known him his whole life, and Raskol told him he'd been with his father when King Boris got shot. With his last breath, the king had told Raskol to get out of France."

Bess took a deep breath. "And he asked his friend to take . . . some important things with him to Cass."

The royal jewels, the ones that were smuggled out of Panaslava, Nancy realized. That's what had been in the briefcase Raskol was carrying.

"It wasn't as though Cass had run away from home," Bess said. "He wrote to his family, and they wrote to him. He just felt he had to get out on his own. To be someone other than an heir to a nonexistent throne."

"So, I don't suppose Cass was delighted to get this latest royal message," Nancy said to Bess.

"No." Her friend shook her head. "He really

wanted no part of what he called his father's 'royal dreams.' Cass was happy here in America. And it looked as though his band was on the verge of success."

"But he had to hear what happened to his father," Nancy said. "And to do that, he had to listen to the rest of what Raskol had to say."

Bess nodded. "They went to Raskol's motel. The guy was pleading with Cass to publicly acknowledge that he was the heir to the throne and to become the king in exile. He told him King Boris had been in the middle of something important for the future of Panaslava."

Nancy remembered Leo Pekary's words. "He was going to act as a middleman to set up talks between the warring factions."

"Anyway, they were interrupted. A guy came into the hotel room and went for Cass with a knife. Raskol jumped in the way and tried to wrestle with him. Instead, he got stabbed."

A loyal subject to the end, Nancy thought. He gave his life for his prince. Even if the prince didn't want the job.

"There was blood all over," Bess went on quietly.

"I know," Nancy said. "Cass stepped in some. The crime scene photos showed a bloody boot print. . . ."

Bess swallowed hard. "All I know is that Cass managed to get away, and he's been hiding ever since."

"What does he want?" Nancy asked.

Bess glared at her friend. "What makes you think he wants something?"

"Cass went to some trouble to track you down and talk to you," Nancy said, surprised by the sudden coldness in her friend's tone. "Okay, I'm sure he wanted you to hear his side of the story, but I think he also needs help. So what does he want? Or, more to the point, Bess, what does he want from you?"

"He wants to get out of here!" Bess's voice was raw as she cried the words. "He wants out of River Heights and out of America. He asked me—begged me—to help him disappear."

Bess sounded brokenhearted. "Cass needs a lift to Chicago. From there, he hopes to make his way to Canada."

Out of here and out of her life, Nancy thought. "And what did you say?"

Bess swiveled in her seat. "I told Cass I'd help him get away—and you can just stay out of it, Nancy."

Chapter

Eighteen

NANCY AND BESS STARED at each other for a long moment. Then Nancy started the car and continued to drive her friend home. Neither girl spoke as they traveled the short distance to Bess's house.

When the car rolled to a stop, Bess opened her door. "I mean it, Nancy," she warned. "Don't try to stop me."

Nancy merely nodded. She wasn't about to make any promises she might have to break. Bess's lips were set in a tight, angry line as she grabbed her bag and stormed out of the car and into her house.

Nancy sat behind the wheel of her car, staring blankly out the side window as the Marvins' front door slammed. Okay, she thought. Bess obviously isn't going to let herself be talked out of helping Cass. So what do I do now? I could call the cops in. But if they take Cass to jail, I might as well paint a target on his forehead for the Haiduk. I could tell Mr. and Mrs. Marvin what Bess is up to and simply write off Bess's friendship, at least for a good, long time. I could . . .

She shook her head. I could spend the whole afternoon playing this game.

Instead, Nancy decided to drive her car to the garage to have a new tire put on and have the spare fixed.

While the tire was being replaced, she had lunch. When her car was ready, Nancy went around town doing errands. When she couldn't invent any more errands, she drove around aimlessly for a while.

Her plan didn't work, though. Try as she might, she couldn't forget about Bess and Cass and the mess they were in.

When Nancy realized she was passing the motel where the Hardys were staying, for the third time, she stopped the car. It's a sign, she thought. Her subconscious mind must be giving her a hint.

Frank and Joe were just on their way out the door when Nancy drove up.

"Just the person we need," Joe said. "We're going to grab a quick early supper and could use you to tell us where to go."

"We'd like your company, too, of course," Frank added.

"Could you hold off for a couple of minutes?" Nancy asked. "There's something I need to talk to you about."

Frank and Joe went back into their room and sat down. Nancy paced as she explained about the phone call Bess received from Cass Carroll and Bess's plan to help him escape.

"I can't talk to Bess," Nancy concluded. "I can't talk to her parents, and I can't talk to the cops."

Frank rubbed his chin. "The one you should really talk to is Cass Carroll. But the only way you can get to him is to follow Bess when she makes her move."

"Which will probably be tonight," Joe added. "If he hasn't moved already."

Now Nancy felt really guilty.

"Forget it," Frank said. "They won't take off till it's dark. I guess we have a change in plans if we're staking out Bess's house."

"Right," Joe said. "For one thing, we'll have to get our supper to go."

"I think we should stop by the car rental place for a new set of wheels," Frank said. "Bess has seen the car we're driving."

The new-car smell of the Hardys' replacement car was buried under the scent of cheeseburgers, onion rings, and french fries. In the neighborhood around them, lights were going out one by one. But the lights were still on at the Marvins'.

Frank had chosen a good spot for the stakeout.

They were parked under a tree that cut off the glow of the streetlights. Their positioning hid not only the car but also the three people sitting inside, watching and waiting.

Even so, Nancy and her friends stayed low in their seats.

Nancy filled Frank and Joe in on the Marvins' usual routine. "They like to watch the late news, then catch the opening monologue on one of the late-night shows," she explained. That meant it would almost be midnight before the family killed the lights and went to bed.

"You called it," Joe said as the living-room lights went off at eleven-fifty.

Soon the whole house was dark. If Bess was going to make her move then, it all came down to one thing. How long would she wait for her parents to fall asleep?

The answer was, not long. It was barely five minutes past midnight when the front door opened and a blond-haired figure dressed in black scuttled down the drive.

"She's picked up a few undercover moves from you, Nancy," Joe said. "She's got the dark clothes and has her car parked ready to go on the street."

"She should have worn a cap or something, though," Nancy said. "Her hair is like a blond beacon."

Instead of starting her engine, Bess coasted down a slight incline until she was several yards from her house. Frank waited until she was almost a block ahead of them before starting his car.

It was a slow-speed chase. Bess was careful to stay below the speed limit, obviously not wanting to attract the attention of the local police.

Nancy found the pursuit nerve-wracking, but it had to be worse for Frank as driver. He couldn't let Bess get too far ahead, because a red light or a truck getting between them could allow her to escape. But if he got too close, Bess might spot him and get spooked. Then they'd never find Cass.

Nancy couldn't tear her eyes from the scarlet taillights of Bess's car. Where would she lead them? Would there be time to confront Cass Carroll? How would he react to their intervention?

"Well, the neighborhood's familiar," Joe said, breaking into Nancy's thoughts.

She looked around. They were back in Little Panaslava, traveling through a maze of side streets. Bess drove even more slowly, apparently searching for landmarks. Finally, she brought her car to a stop at the entrance to a dark alley.

Frank killed his lights and glided to a stop on the deserted street. "She's out and walking down the alley," he announced.

"She must really like this guy," Joe said. "*I* wouldn't like to walk down there alone at midnight."

"We've got to get closer," Nancy said. "She could walk through a door and disappear."

In an instant, Nancy, Frank, and Joe were out of the car and across the street.

They could hear Bess's footsteps on the pavement, echoing off the brick walls. She should be wearing sneakers, Nancy thought.

Moving as quickly but silently as possible, Nancy and the Hardys followed a safe distance behind Bess. Ahead, Nancy could make out the glimmer of a streetlight. They must have cut right through the block.

Bess suddenly stopped, and they could hear her rap her knuckles against something solid and metallic. Nancy, Frank, and Joe froze in the shadows as a bright rectangle of light flashed on the right-hand wall of the alley—a doorway. A tall, black silhouette took Bess by the arm and led her in.

Nancy sprinted from her hiding place. She heard more running footfalls as the Hardys followed close behind. The big, heavy door had almost swung shut when she reached it. Grabbing at the knob, Nancy flung the door back. She confronted the square of bright light, shadows—and, she suddenly realized, delicious smells.

Bess stared with wide eyes, her mouth hanging open in shock. Beside her stood a silver-haired man.

"Egon!" Nancy cried in surprise.

Egon Marek's face was pale and strained as he peered out at Nancy and the Hardys. For once, he wasn't wearing one of his impeccable double-breasted jackets but a baggy old cardigan sweater. He didn't speak to Nancy but immediately turned to Bess. "You were supposed to tell no one," Egon scolded.

"I didn't," Bess answered.

"I knew Cass was in touch with Bess," Nancy said. "We just followed her."

"Well, in, in." Egon shepherded Nancy and the Hardys from the delivery entrance into the kitchen. "No sense letting all the heat out."

"You've been hiding Cass all along," Frank said shrewdly.

Egon nodded. "From the moment we met, I recognized young Casimir. He looks very much like his grandfather. The hair is longer, his clothes, the silly, sloppy style some young people wear," the old aristocrat said. "But I knew he was my prince."

He smiled. "And I have seen some photos of Prince Casimir in magazines over the years."

"So that's why you hid him from the cops," Frank thought out loud.

Again, Egon shrugged, as if he did this sort of thing every day.

"But how did you keep him hidden during the big search?" Nancy had to know.

The aristocratic old man pointed to the wall of the kitchen. Three ovens stood open. "The cooking was being done, remember?" he said. "Two ovens were on. The middle one was off."

"Even so, I nearly roasted," Cass Carroll said as he walked into the room, carrying two large, heavy garbage bags. He was dressed in a kitchen helper's stained white uniform, and his long hair had been chopped off.

"Cass?" Bess cried in disbelief.

He looked at Bess with a rueful grin. "Clothes sure do make the man, don't they? On the other hand, the uniform has been pretty useful. Who pays much attention to the pot scourer and garbage man?"

"You served the coffee when I came here to apologize to Dedya Egon!" Nancy exclaimed. Cass nodded.

Joe leaned over and spoke in Nancy's ear, "You didn't recognize him?"

"Cass," Nancy began, ignoring Joe's snide remark. "Um, Prince Casimir, these are my friends, Frank and Joe Hardy."

"Call me Cass, please," the young man replied. "This prince stuff has never been anything but trouble. I've always loathed it." He shook hands with the boys. "Egon has spoken of you, and so has Bess."

"We knew Bess would be trying to smuggle you out of town." Nancy tried to ignore her friend's glare. "Nobody knows we're here—not the cops, not Bess's parents. We just want to talk to you for a moment, to beg you to reconsider—"

"Too late," a voice interrupted her.

The swinging door from the empty restaurant opened, and a shiny, nickel-plated automatic gun poked through—pointed right at Cass's head.

Then the rest of the gunmen followed.

Nancy gasped. It was Tad Vlachovic!

"You don't know what you're doing, Tadeusz," Egon began.

The older man paled as the gun was swung up and leveled at his face.

"Shut up, you old fool!" Tad spat on the kitchen floor.

Nancy, Joe, and Frank tensed, ready to exploit the first opportunity to jump the young thug. But they couldn't do anything while Egon was covered. At such close range, Tad couldn't miss.

"Just like a fairy tale," Tad mocked. "A prince. You weren't the only one keeping an eye on your girlfriend," he said, leering at Nancy.

Joe was disgusted with himself. "Should have kept an eye out for other tails."

"Too late now," Tad told him. "Prince Casimir is worth real money to certain people. And then there's the gold you're carrying. Where is it, Princie?"

"I don't know what you're talking about," Cass replied, staring into Tad's eyes.

"I'm talking about how your blue-blooded buddy here will get shot if you don't turn that gold over—now." Tad thrust his pistol at Egon while staying out of his reach.

"Okay, everybody, on the floor. Sit on your hands," the punk ordered.

The line came right out of a recent movie. The move seemed silly, but once they did it, they'd be almost helpless, unable to move quickly.

Bess sat down first. Her eyes never left Cass.

Egon followed more slowly. So did Cass. Nancy, Frank, and Joe were the most reluctant. Tad went to the door and opened it. His big buddy and the zit-faced kid came in.

"I don't have to shoot the old egghead right away," Tad told Cass. "We can hurt him a little, first. Porky here"—he nodded to the muscular guy—"used to work for McBurgers, until they fired him. Your host won't look quite as handsome after Porky grills his face medium rare."

Tad glanced from the shining kitchen grill to the big, bulky guy. Porky moved toward Egon, but Cass spoke up.

"I'll show you," he said.

Tad gestured for him to rise. Cass stood and went to a pile of flour bags. These weren't the usual five-pound size that Hannah bought for the Drew kitchen. They were the size of a doormat and five inches thick. After a little shifting, Cass revealed the bottom row. One bag was sealed with tape.

Ripping the bag open, Cass scooped up a handful of flour. His shoulders tensed.

"Uh-uh-uh," Tad warned. "Don't do something stupid."

Cass bent over the bag, spilling out the flour. There was something else inside—a briefcase sealed in plastic.

Tad seized the case as Cass freed it, obviously not minding the white dust that dribbled around him. He scooped out the crown, a golden circlet set with jewels, while letting the briefcase clank to the floor. "Beautiful," he said, admiring the crown. "These sparklers are a bonus."

"You can't destroy them!" Cass cried in shock.

"Worried about your royal inheritance?" Tad mocked.

"This isn't about royalty," Cass said. "They represent the history of Panaslava."

"It's about both," Egon insisted. "Kings represent most of our nation's history." He muttered. "Just as most of it was Vlachovic betraying Ladinovic."

"Wake up, you stupid old fossil," Tad snarled. "I couldn't care less about your dumb feuds in the moldy old country. I'm an American now, and I'm doing this for money—lots of it."

Keeping his gun trained on Egon, Tad, with his thuggish friends, forced the prisoners outside and into a beat-up van.

"I thought it was illegal to paint over the back windows," Joe said.

"Whoops! Stop the kidnapping," Tad mocked. "Our van isn't up to code."

The captives jounced along inside the boxy space with no idea where they were going. Abruptly, the van stopped, and the horn sounded—two short beeps followed by one long one. Nancy heard the rattling sound of a metal gate being raised. The van moved forward, then stopped. "Everybody out," Tad Vlachovic ordered.

They found themselves in a dingy warehouse, where a single hanging bulb threw a wan circle of illumination. The light was enough, though, for Nancy to make out the face of Leo Pekary.

The businessman had been sitting on a large crate, sipping coffee from a paper cup. He was not very happy about what he saw. "Who are all these?" he demanded of Tad Vlachovic. "I didn't ask you to invite the whole neighborhood."

"Witnesses," Tad replied briefly. "I figured you'd want them along—for a modest extra fee."

"Just more people to get rid of," Pekary grunted.

"You're the Haiduk?" Joe Hardy demanded in disbelief.

Pekary laughed in his face. "No, I'm the man who will save Sarabia. They wouldn't listen to me in the elections. But they'll need me—and my money—in this war." His eyes gleamed with a fanatical light. "I can save our people, and our brothers in the other so-called republics. In time a greater Sarabia will take the place of a fragmented Panaslava."

"But you need war to do that," Nancy said. "And King Boris got in your way by trying to arrange a peace treaty."

Pekary gave her a shrewd look. "Exactly, young lady. My supporters in Europe took care of that foolish princeling. While here, I hired the Haiduk."

He stepped aside. "Take them!"

Another figure appeared from the shadows, cutting them off from the closed garage door. Nancy didn't recognize the assault rifle in the man's hands.

But she recognized the man.

She knew him as Chuck Bascomb.

Chapter

Nineteen

J OE HARDY GLARED at the assault gun in Bascomb's hands. "I guess a Soviet-trained assassin *would* use an AK-47."

Bascomb gave him a thin smile. "Oh, this is the next generation, the AK-74. No shoulder stock, lighter bullets, and more of them. I could put four shots in every person in this room."

Tad Vlachovic gestured with his shiny pistol. "Hey, I don't like you counting me and the boys as targets. Just give us what we've got coming to us, and we're out of here."

The muzzle of Bascomb's light machine gun moved to cover the punk. "Oh, you'll get exactly what you deserve. Now, put the gun down."

"No way," Tad replied. "You gave me this piece, I'm keepin' it. I got plans for it."

"This isn't a game, boy. No finders keepers, no

do-overs. I gave you an order. Put the gun down."

Instead, Tad raised and aimed the pistol at Bascomb's face in his best TV-bad-guy style, gun in his right hand, left hand on his right wrist. "Make me."

Joe looked back and forth between the two. At this range, Bascomb's assault rifle would tear Tad in two. But any shot Tad got off would likely hit Bascomb—the Haiduk—too.

Tad's face was pale as he realized the assassin was serious. "I wouldn't have minded putting a bullet in Old Egon or Princie-poo here," he said, his voice loud with false bravado. "I can put one in you, too, even with your fancy gun. Just give me my money—"

Joe took a step forward. The muzzle of the Haiduk's weapon veered to cover him.

Tad Vlachovic fired!

Even in the cavernous room, the gunshot was deafening. But Joe heard Tad Vlachovic's scream, rather than the Haiduk's. The shattered remains of his shiny pistol clattered to the floor as Tad clamped his left hand over his bloody right one and dropped to his knees, shrieking in pain.

"You rigged his gun to blow up, and then you gave it to him." Joe stared at Bascomb—no, he reminded himself, at the Haiduk.

"I doctored it myself," the assassin admitted with pride. "A pretty toy to give to a disposable tool."

Porky and the zit-faced thug stood frozen, their faces pale, as their leader groveled on the floor.

"I really have to compliment you on your English," Frank spoke up. "You even have our slang down pat. That must be tough for a native Rurithenian."

The Haiduk shrugged. More and more of Chuck Bascomb slid from his face, like a mask he no longer needed. "It was necessary to make me a better agent," he said. "One has to fit in, especially with the work I do."

"Oh, yes," Frank agreed. "A good cover is everything."

"For instance," the Haiduk went on, "I paid special attention to how your government works while I was working in Washington, D.C. There is"—he gave them a chilling smile—"or, rather, there *was* an actual State Department man named Chuck Bascomb investigating me. His files mentioned Nancy Drew, while my country's files mentioned the work you and your brother have sometimes done for your government— and your connection with Ms. Drew."

Even though the Haiduk was glancing at Nancy, the barrel of the AK-74 swung to cover Joe.

"You can stop right there, Mr. Hardy. I haven't missed your attempt to get closer—those little steps while your brother was talking. And you can be sure I won't miss if you take another one."

Joe froze, frustrated. He knew that Frank had been trying to buy time so that someone could attempt a move. But Joe was still yards away from the hired killer. That was too far away to take down someone with an assault rifle, especially when the weapon was aimed at him.

"But enough conversation. Talking before killing is not a good idea." The Haiduk's tone was almost casual, as if what he was about to do was somehow boring. "It's time for me to do the job I was hired for. Although," he added with a glance at Leo Pekary, "I'm afraid my fee has gone up in the last hour. I was engaged to eliminate Prince Casimir only. Witnesses were not part of our original agreement. I'm afraid it will cost you, Mr. Pekary."

Leo Pekary glanced at the prisoners as if they were so many trees to be cut down and cleared out of his way. He was ruthless, but he hadn't become rich by indulging every little desire.

"Exactly how much more?" Pekary asked.

The Haiduk almost turned his gun on his wealthy employer but knew too well that any glitch in covering this crowd could mean failure.

"You fat, petit bourgeois dictator with no country! You are talking to the Haiduk, idiot. I do not haggle over money. Either I kill them all for my price, or I kill them and then you."

"Perhaps . . ." Pekary began.

Barely moving a muscle, the Haiduk refocused and shot a line in front of Pekary's feet before aiming the gun back at Joe. No one had moved, not even Pekary.

"Don't cross that line!" the Haiduk ordered the man who had hired him.

"Kill them," Pekary said, visibly shaken but trying to regain his composure. "I've got more important things to take care of."

"Oh, yes." Egon's smile was bitterly ironic. "What are a few inconvenient human beings?"

Pekary glared at the old man. "I know the dangers of humanitarian impulses, Mr. Marek. It was decisions made for the good of the people that brought Sarabia—Panaslava—to the sorry state she is presently in."

"And all this time, I thought it was merely a few bloody-handed idiots, stirring up the people's hatreds and fears," Egon responded, his voice like a lash.

"The country needs leadership," Pekary said. "It was timidity and weakness in high places that allowed Panaslava to fall apart. I can remedy that."

"The people wouldn't have you as a leader. That's why they didn't elect you."

"Several factions accept my money, and my advice now. Already I control things from behind the scenes. As the war continues, they will need my money even more. I will dictate the course the patriots take, until a strong new Sarabia occupies the fragmented lands of the old, weak Panaslava. Then we can seize the lands stolen from us by the Bulgarians and Greeks—"

"And start an even bigger war," Egon cut in.

"Careful you don't bankrupt yourself, Mr. Pekary."

It seemed that Pekary hardly heard him, so hypnotized was he by his dreams of glory. "A true leader needs no election. He follows the march of history."

"With the help of an assassin to clear the parade route."

Pekary aimed a venomous look at Egon. "Most amusing. We'll see if you continue to laugh when your precious prince dies." He gestured to the assassin.

As the Haiduk switched and aimed his weapon at Cass Carroll, Joe noticed that the killer's face continued to wear a slightly bored smile, but his eyes were now gleaming.

To Joe, everything seemed to be moving in slow motion.

Cass—or Prince Casimir—drew himself up in an effort to meet his death with some sense of dignity. Tad Vlachovic crouched, still moaning. His assistants stood flat-footed, scared spitless.

Nancy had all her weight on her toes, ready to leap. From the way she was studying Cass, Joe figured she'd try to tackle him out of the line of fire. Frank looked ready to run at the gunman. Joe, a step or two closer, prepared to do the same.

Not that they had much hope of stopping the killer. Bascomb had told the truth about one thing. That gun could fire almost eleven rounds a second.

The last thing Joe expected was a gunshot— from *behind* him.

Startled, he glanced over his shoulder. From out of his ratty old sweater, Egon had produced a pistol. It was an old-style Luger, a weapon from World War II.

But the gun was still lethal after all these years.

Egon's shot caught the Haiduk in the arm. The hired killer's teeth showed in a grimace of pain as he spun away from the impact of the bullet.

But he was a pro. He didn't drop his gun. The AK-74 swung up, and a three-shot burst shattered the single light fixture.

Blackness fell over them like a stifling rug. Wild cries and running footsteps echoed in the empty warehouse.

Joe hurled himself at the spot where the Haiduk had been standing. The killer wasn't there now.

A second later a body smashed into him. Hands grabbed his arm in a hold for throwing.

Abruptly, Joe stopped struggling. Unarmed combat? This couldn't be the Haiduk. The assassin had a gun. "Frank?" he said.

"Joe?" An embarrassed voice answered out of the darkness.

The Hardy brothers dove for the floor as another quick burst of automatic fire hammered their ears.

Joe kept his eyes open, facing the glaring muzzle flash. He crawled across the floor toward the gunman's position.

But again the killer was gone by the time Joe got there.

Someone—Porky, by the weight of him—stepped on Joe as he ran through the darkness. Joe could tell that the invisible runner staggered but managed to keep his feet. A second later came the sounds of someone fumbling at the steel garage door.

The Haiduk's AK-74 yammered again, and there was a scream. Whatever happened to Porky, he wouldn't be attempting to open the door anymore.

"Be careful," a scared, furious voice burst out. Joe recognized Leo Pekary. "You almost hit me."

"Then stay out of my way," the Haiduk shouted angrily.

Joe could understand that the killer might be a little annoyed. A straightforward execution had suddenly turned into a life-and-death game of devil in the dark—or was it blindman's bluff?

The Haiduk had the firepower. But he no longer had his sights on the targets. And unless Pekary was willing to join in the fight, he was grossly outnumbered. Faced with death, even the punks would turn against the men who'd hired them. Although, Joe had to admit, Tad wouldn't be much help now. And it sounded as if Porky was out of the fight, as well.

The professional killer had only spent three shots. He still had more than thirty bullets available. And, Joe suspected, he was probably carrying another curved clip of forty bullets for his gun.

Old Egon, if his gun were fully loaded, had only seven shots left. He was obviously hoarding his bullets, waiting for a sure hit. The old man must be used to fighting in night conditions.

Somebody in the darkness ran into a box, resulting in a crash and a shouted "Oof!"

Another set of three shots rattled out, followed by a single *boom!* from Egon's Luger. Then came a longer burst from the assault rifle, as the Haiduk aimed for the pistol's flash.

Sure, Joe realized, the Haiduk is a pro. His first priority is to take out the only other person with a gun.

He scuttled low along the floor, trying to catch the killer before he moved away again. But again Joe found himself pouncing on empty space.

This guy is good, he thought. *Very* good. Even that's an understatement. He moves too quietly for me to hear, even with a bullet hole in one arm.

Joe concentrated on making some soundless movement himself. He didn't want to be the next one to draw fire.

How many shots did the Haiduk have left? Twenty? Twenty-five?

A scream shattered the lightless space. Nancy? Joe shook his head, even as Leo Pekary's voice rang out. "Don't shoot! I've got the girlfriend!"

Joe aimed himself for the shouts and the sounds of struggle.

Pekary cried out in pain and yelled something in Sarabian. It didn't sound like a compliment, Joe thought.

Then Pekary switched to English. "The little witch kicked me—" There was a loud thunk as Pekary fell to the ground, groaning in anguish.

Joe tried to listen for the sound of Bess's footsteps. But they were almost impossible to distinguish among the other noises in the total blackness.

Then came a pained grunt, the sound of scuffling, and another scream from Bess: "Nooooo!"

"Hold still!" a voice snapped.

Joe's blood froze in his veins. That was the voice of Chuck Bascomb—the Haiduk!

Bess screamed again in the darkness, this time in pain.

"I said, hold *still!*" the harsh, grating voice ordered.

The scuffling stopped, but Joe could hear little whimpers coming from Bess. He has Bess, Joe thought.

"All right," the Haiduk said, his voice more confident. "Ms. Marvin got away from Mr. Pekary, but she blundered into me. I have her held quite securely, and my weapon is pointed at her head. Just one flinch, and—"

A choking sound came from Bess.

He must have her in a headlock, Joe figured.

"I understand you're quite fond of this young woman, Prince Casimir," the Haiduk went on, as if cries of fear were regular interruptions in his conversations. "Well, we'll see how far you're willing to go for her."

The voice in the darkness grew cold. As he paused, everyone was entirely motionless and silent.

"Because, unless you show yourself in ten seconds, Ms. Marvin dies!"

Chapter
Twenty

Nancy Drew was almost completely lost in the darkness. The glow from the streetlight that seeped in from the outside was barely enough to outline some shuttered windows. She must have gotten completely turned around in the commotion since that last orgy of shooting. Where was the door they'd entered through?

But now she had no thoughts for opening an escape route. With Bess in the clutches of a coldblooded killer, she had more pressing issues at hand. She could hear the sound of Bess gasping, but she couldn't tell exactly where the noise was coming from yet.

The second after the Haiduk made his threat, Cass Carroll's voice rang out. "How am I supposed to show myself when we're all effectively blind?"

The killer was silent for a moment. Then he called, "Mr. Pekary, do you remember the large crate you were sitting on?"

"Of course," the Panaslav faction leader replied.

"I left a flashlight on it—just in case," the Haiduk said. "Could you find it and turn it on?"

As she listened to the fumbling search, Nancy thought that if she could find it first she could break it.

The beam of the light suddenly appeared, blinding everyone used to the darkness. Nancy blinked and raised a hand to shield her eyes.

Pekary tossed the flashlight, which went rolling across the floor. Its fan of radiance caught Nancy's legs. She immediately dove away from the light, to cheat the Haiduk of another target.

"Very good, Ms. Drew." The Haiduk's chuckle echoed from the shadows. "But you're not the one I want."

"Yet," Nancy added from where she was crouched on the floor. "Once you kill Cass, you've got to kill us all."

"He's got to kill us, anyway." Frank Hardy's angry voice came from somewhere off to her left. "We've seen his face. We know who the Haiduk is—his cover is blown."

"Silence," the assassin demanded. "Enough discussion." Nancy took a few steps forward, trying to follow the sound of his voice.

"You asked how you could show yourself, Prince Casimir," the Haiduk said. "It's quite simple, Your Highness. All you need to do is stand in the light of the flashlight."

Nancy heard footsteps on the concrete floor headed toward the flashlight.

"Cass! Don't!" Bess screamed. "He'll kill you!"

"Casimir, you mustn't!" Egon begged. "My prince—"

"What sort of prince lets his friends die to save himself?" Cass replied.

He stepped into the light, and in spite of his stained kitchen uniform, Cass Carroll looked every inch the prince. "You've got me now. Let Bess go."

"Yes, I thought I could depend on your sense of chivalry," the Haiduk said. "Forgive me if I hold on to Ms. Marvin a little longer—just until my job is finished."

Nancy suddenly caught the glint of light off oiled metal. She strained her eyes, trying to make the most of the feeble glow from the flashlight.

Yes! There was the AK-74 gun barrel. That vague shape to the left of it must be Bess. And behind the metallic shine, really a point of light like a star in the night sky, a large figure hovered. The more Nancy looked, the clearer the pair in the shadows became. The Haiduk held on to Bess with his left arm around her neck. He also had a handful of her long blond hair, tilting her head toward the ceiling. He still held the assault rifle in his right hand, even though that arm was the one with the bullet in it.

Of course, Nancy realized. He'd use his un-damaged arm to hold Bess in line.

Nancy dashed through the shadows, careful not to silhouette herself against the light shining on Cass. She was still too far away as the gun was moved to cover the prince.

But as soon as the muzzle was turned away from her head, Bess's shadowy form twisted. Yelling at the top of her lungs, she rammed both fists down onto the Haiduk's wounded gun arm.

The assassin roared like an injured wild beast, while Bess gave a war cry. Then both were drowned out as a burst of fire from the assault rifle shattered the floor, nowhere near Cass. Bess had managed to deflect the Haiduk's aim with her desperate attack.

He must be pretty tough, Nancy thought as she charged forward. Even though Bess punched his wounded arm, he still managed to hold on to his gun.

They were wrestling now, Bess frantically trying to keep the assault rifle from turning on either her or Cass. But the Haiduk was stronger—and ruthless. With his hand still twined in Bess's long hair, he shook her the way a cat shakes a mouse. She lost her grip.

Holding her out at arm's length, the assassin brought up his gun—

When a figure came hurtling from the shadows to tackle him!

Nancy winced as Bess screamed again in pain.

The Haiduk was knocked to the floor, but he pulled Bess along with him—by the hair.

A quick glimpse of short blond hair told Nancy that Joe Hardy was the one who'd taken down the killer.

The problem was, the killer refused to stay down. He seemed unstoppable.

Releasing Bess, the Haiduk caught Joe under the chin with the palm of his hand, forcing his face toward the ceiling and his body to arch backward. Then the Haiduk swung his assault rifle, whacking Joe in the side of the head.

Joe lurched, and the Haiduk sent him toppling. Slithering like an eel, the assassin moved across the floor and leaped to his feet. He was bringing his gun around as Nancy arrived. She lashed out with her foot, trying to kick the weapon out of the Haiduk's grasp.

He must have gotten some sort of warning, because he spun the weapon out of the way and smashed back with a high kick of his own.

There was no way Nancy could block. All she could do was try to protect herself. She took the kick on her hip and tumbled to the floor just as Joe had done.

Her self-defense classes had taught her how to fall, but even so, Nancy landed hard. The wind was knocked out of her, and she was gasping for air as she tried to roll back onto her feet. Even as she moved, the Haiduk whipped his weapon around to aim at her.

Nancy flung herself in the opposite direction

in a frantic scramble. Then Frank Hardy entered the battle. She could see him clearly, because the wild, swirling fight had taken them into the cone of light flung by the flashlight.

Frank's face was grim and furious as he tried for a takedown hold on the Haiduk. But his opponent showed his martial arts skill and experience once again.

The assassin twisted free, bringing his gun around to finish Frank off.

By then Joe Hardy had lurched back into the fight. He was on his knees and clearly woozy, but he grabbed for the assault rifle.

He didn't get a clear grip, but the Haiduk's scream was as much from pain as from fury. He snatched his gun away, whirled with his leg high in a roundhouse kick, and smashed into Frank.

The older Hardy seemed to fly through the air—and he landed on Joe. The two brothers sprawled on the floor half-stunned, trying to move but only getting in each other's way. Over them, the Haiduk bared his teeth in a grimace of triumph, aiming his gun.

Preoccupied with the Hardys, he never saw Nancy spin across the floor, her leg aiming for the back of his left knee. Direct hit.

She almost bounced back from the impact as she battered his leg out from under him. The Haiduk toppled like a chopped-down tree.

He landed heavily on his back, his right hand outflung. But as Nancy wobbled to her feet, she saw he still kept his grip on the gun. In fact, the

Haiduk was still struggling to bring his weapon to bear when a heavy motorcycle boot landed on his forearm.

The assassin's hand smacked down to the concrete, and the weapon went clattering away.

Cass Carroll kept the pressure up on the wounded arm. The Haiduk writhed like an insect held in place by a pin. He got his left leg under him and tried to throw a blow, but Frank Hardy blocked that, twisting the arm back. The man tried to kick, but Joe Hardy pounced on his legs.

As Nancy rose to her feet, holding the flashlight now, Egon stepped forward, aiming his Luger at the trapped assassin. "I'm thinking maybe it's time *you* held still," the old man said.

From behind, they heard an angry, whiny voice yell, "Hey, where do you think *you're* going, bozo?"

Nancy shifted the flashlight to illuminate both the prone Haiduk and the struggle going on in the darkness nearby. By the time she had them lit, Tad Vlachovic's zit-faced companion had a choke hold on Leo Pekary.

"If you guys can keep a lid on things, I'll see if I can find a phone," Nancy said. "This looks like a job for the police."

Chief McGinnis shook his head as his officers took away the patched-up Haiduk and Pekary. "It seems incredible that a man with so much going for him would risk it all on such a crazy plot."

Nancy shrugged. "Leo Pekary saw himself as something more than a businessman—a ruler of men, maybe even a dictator. From what I've been hearing, things in the old Panaslav republics are so chaotic, his plans might have succeeded."

"And the government agent who came to warn us of an assassination turns out to be the assassin himself." The chief looked a little shell-shocked.

"Well, it explains the weird attitude 'Bascomb' adopted as we began to find out things about Cass," Nancy said.

"And it was a pretty elaborate scheme he created to come to River Heights," Joe added.

"Yeah," Nancy said. "Most people fly into Chicago and rent a car to drive here."

That got a chuckle from the local constabulary. "Apparently," began Joe, "the Haiduk murdered the real Chuck Bascomb and assumed his identity. Then he enlisted our help, because we're always willing to help out the feds."

"He used you to get into our confidence here, through Nancy," the chief said, venturing into the story.

"He must have expected to catch Cass quickly," Frank continued. "And nearly did, the first night, after we saw Cass and Raskol in the car. But Raskol foiled that attempt, and Cass escaped, leaving him stuck here, and—well, you know the rest."

The chief shook his head. "I know this case

would have been real trouble if it hadn't been for you and your friends."

"Or, from another point of view," Frank said, "if Bascomb hadn't contacted us and so hadn't met Nancy—and Bess—this might have been a much quieter crime."

Nancy glanced over at the battered and bruised Hardys. "Maybe it would have been quieter, but it could easily have become more devastating." Nancy turned back to Chief McGinnis. "We were glad to help." She put her hands on her hips and winced. It felt as if she'd have a good-size bruise of her own the next day.

She joined Frank and Joe, who had formed an amused audience as Cass alternately fussed over Bess and scolded Egon.

"You could have gotten yourself killed, pulling out that old cannon," the prince told the café proprietor.

Egon's reply was a shrug. "Years ago your grandfather kept me from marching off to Panaslava and getting killed. I owe my life to a Ladinovic. If I should die saving another Ladinovic, it would only be fair."

"I'm not a real Ladinovic," Cass protested.

"You have the blood of one, and you acted like one," Egon said. "You stepped into the light rather than let Bess die. You even called yourself a prince."

"I know what you're saying, Egon." Cass looked at the old man sternly.

213

Egon shrugged his shoulders in innocence.

"You're saying that there's no getting away from it," Cass said, his voice low.

"After all this publicity?" Egon asked.

Cass sighed, looking at Bess. "No hope for a private life."

"Rock stars don't have private lives any more than princes do," Bess said.

"That is a good point," Cass admitted. He drew himself up straight. "But rock stars do not have the responsibilities of a prince. I know now that when this mess is cleared up, I'll have to return to Paris. I'll try to get my father's peace talks back on track somehow."

"That might be easier than you think," Frank suggested. "When people hear what Pekary's faction was up to, you may be able to embarrass some of the other players at the peace table."

Prince Casimir nodded. "And after that— well, all this publicity should be good for my first album. I know a princess who balances a singing career against her royal obligations. So I should be able to come back." He grinned at Bess, who gave him a small, shy smile.

"If you remember me," she said.

"You think I'd forget the woman who saved my life? No way." Cass flung an arm around Bess, holding her close. "Whatever happens, we'll always have River Heights."

Bess snuggled closer. "I'd rather have Paris."

The two of them wandered over to a quiet

corner while the police finished up their work on the scene.

"So, boys," Nancy began. "Whose case was this, anyway?"

"What do you mean?" Frank asked. "We all worked on it. It's our case."

"I'm just wondering, you know, percentages," Nancy replied. "Let's see, I got the theory that Cass was royalty and the theory that the Haiduk was after him."

"My theory was that Cass was the Haiduk," Joe said, sounding miserable. Then he perked up. "But Frank and I had that incredible rooftop race, risking life and limb—"

"To catch the wrong guy," Nancy reminded him. "Doesn't count. I spotted Tad Vlachovic driving Pekary's car, so we knew Pekary wasn't legit."

"Can't give you that one, Nancy," Frank said. "You only thought you saw him. We weren't sure he was involved until tonight."

"Okay, okay," Nancy replied. "But I found the strongbox with the passport in it."

"Wrong again, Nancy," Joe said with a smile. "Bess knew where that was. Meanwhile, we changed your tire, drove you around town, and saved you from Tad Vlachovic that first night in the alley."

Nancy was getting a little steamed.

"Aren't you glad you brought it up?" Frank asked.

The sweethearts strolled back arm in arm. "What's the matter, Nancy?" Bess asked. "You look mad—oh, you're not still angry at me for wanting to help Cass escape, are you?"

Chief McGinnis's ears suddenly perked up. He opened his mouth to say something, but Egon cut him off.

"Mudrashka Natalya!" Old Egon exclaimed. "You should be ashamed of yourself for trying to count who did what, so who solved the—"

"Mudrashka?" Cass asked, laughing.

"What's so funny about that?" Nancy became defensive. "I call Dedya Egon grandfather, and he calls me Mudrashka, granddaughter."

Cass really burst out laughing then, and Nancy saw a sly smile cross Old Egon's face. She felt her own face turning red. Everyone else looked at the three of them blankly.

Through his quieting chuckles, Cass said, "Dedya means grandfather, yes, but mudrashka— granddaughter? No."

Nancy's eyebrows shot up. "*What* have you been calling me? Some dirty old name?" Her voice shook between anger and disappointment.

"No, no, Natalya," Egon said, drawing close to her and putting his hand on her arm. "It was my little joke. Cass tells the truth. *Mudrashka* does not mean granddaughter. It means . . . you might say . . . little wise woman."

Frank and Joe let out whoops of friendly teasing laughter, but Nancy paid no attention to them. She leaned over and kissed Dedya Egon's cheek.

The crowd responded as one, "Aw, Mudrashka."

"My advice is, don't let the words of a senile old expatriate go to your head, Nancy. I want to thank all of you for helping me and having faith in me," Cass said.

"Well, I have a piece of advice for you, too, Cass," Nancy said with a straight face.

Cass, Bess, and the others turned to her.

"What's that?" Cass asked.

"When you become a famous rock star, whatever you do, *don't* use the stage name Prince."

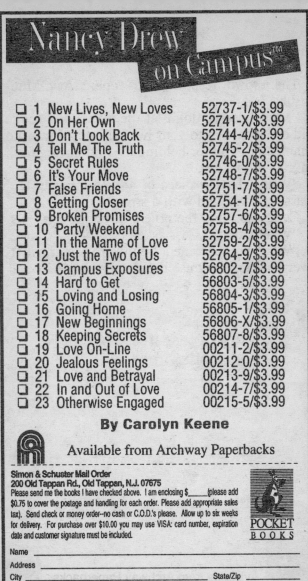

Nancy Drew on Campus™

❏ 1	New Lives, New Loves	52737-1/$3.99
❏ 2	On Her Own	52741-X/$3.99
❏ 3	Don't Look Back	52744-4/$3.99
❏ 4	Tell Me The Truth	52745-2/$3.99
❏ 5	Secret Rules	52746-0/$3.99
❏ 6	It's Your Move	52748-7/$3.99
❏ 7	False Friends	52751-7/$3.99
❏ 8	Getting Closer	52754-1/$3.99
❏ 9	Broken Promises	52757-6/$3.99
❏ 10	Party Weekend	52758-4/$3.99
❏ 11	In the Name of Love	52759-2/$3.99
❏ 12	Just the Two of Us	52764-9/$3.99
❏ 13	Campus Exposures	56802-7/$3.99
❏ 14	Hard to Get	56803-5/$3.99
❏ 15	Loving and Losing	56804-3/$3.99
❏ 16	Going Home	56805-1/$3.99
❏ 17	New Beginnings	56806-X/$3.99
❏ 18	Keeping Secrets	56807-8/$3.99
❏ 19	Love On-Line	00211-2/$3.99
❏ 20	Jealous Feelings	00212-0/$3.99
❏ 21	Love and Betrayal	00213-9/$3.99
❏ 22	In and Out of Love	00214-7/$3.99
❏ 23	Otherwise Engaged	00215-5/$3.99

By Carolyn Keene

Available from Archway Paperbacks

@ café

Meet the staff of @café:
Natalie, Dylan, Blue, Sam, Tanya, and Jason.
They serve coffee, surf the net,
and share their deepest darkest secrets . . .

A brand-new book series coming in November 1997

#1 Love Bytes
It's not just the espresso
that's brewing....

#2 I'll Have What He's Having
It's not the caffeine
that's making everyone jumpy.

Novels by Elizabeth Craft